THE DUKE'S UNEXPECTED HEART

AN ARRANGED MARRIAGE REGENCY ROMANCE

AUBREY TATE

The Duke's Unexpected Heart
An Arranged Marriage Regency Romance
Copyright © 2025 by Aubrey Tate
All rights reserved.

Book Cover and formatting provided by Trisha Fuentes
https://bit.ly/m/trishafuentes

No part of this book may be reproduced in any form or by any electronic or mechanical means, including information storage and retrieval systems, without written permission from the author, except for the use of brief quotations in a book review.

ISBN: 979-8-3493-0264-0 (Paperback)

Published by
Ardent Artist Books
www.ardentartistbooks.com

ABOUT ARDENT ARTIST BOOKS

➥ **ABOUT US**

Ardent Artist Books was established in 2008
We publish modern and historical romances once a month!

Get Your FREE List: Published & Upcoming Books
visit our website at:
https://bit.ly/3Wva4o0

* * *

➥ **WE HAVE BOOK TRAILERS**

Follow us on YouTube!
https://bit.ly/3W3xn7a

Like, Subscribe & Comment

* * *

➥ WE HAVE SERIALIZED FICTION!

Visit our website today to download one of our stories that unfold in bite-sized pieces!

Each installment is just 99¢!
Paperback $15.99

https://bit.ly/3LsDpJL

CONTENTS

1. RAVENSBROOK HALL Yorkshire, England, 1812	1
2. A Meddling Sister	17
3. The Carrington Ball	29
4. The Harsgrove Ball	43
5. The Veranda	55
6. Tempest	67
7. The Sun on Her Face	79
8. Three Stone Dolphins	95
9. Buttercup	111
10. No Dishonor	125
11. Seraphina	139
12. Entanglement	155
13. Spinsters	165
14. A Damp Cloth	177
15. Not Again	189
16. Grass in Your Hair	201
Ten Years Later	211

YOU MIGHT ALSO LIKE

Best-Seller!	227
Ink and Affection	229
A Heart's Wager	231
A Spanish Bride for Strathmore	233
The Auction Rivals	235
About Aubrey	237
Also by Aubrey	239

CHAPTER ONE
RAVENSBROOK HALL
LADY ELEANOR HARTWOOD
YORKSHIRE, ENGLAND, 1812

I sit at our family dinner table, watching my sisters, Victoria and Elizabeth, laugh with their husbands. Victoria's youngest child, Edmund, bounces on her knee, his chubby hands reaching for a silver spoon just beyond his grasp. My other nieces and nephews are at home with their nurses tonight, as Father prefers a more civilized atmosphere for our monthly family dinners at Ravensbrook Hall.

"Edmund has your eyes, Victoria," I say, offering what I hope is a pleasant contribution to the conversation.

Victoria beams. "Everyone says so. Though his temperament is all his father's, thank heavens." She glances adoringly at her husband, the Marquess of Halford, who returns her smile with such warmth that I must look away.

The familiar ache blooms in my chest. Not quite envy—that would be uncharitable—but a longing so profound it sometimes steals my breath. My sisters have everything: beauty, position, love. Victoria, with her golden curls and azure eyes, captured one of the most eligible bachelors in London during her first Season. Elizabeth, whose dark beauty turns heads wherever she goes, married the Earl of Devonham after a courtship that set all of London talking.

And I... I have my music.

"Eleanor, do pass the salt," Father says, interrupting my thoughts. "No use staring into space. Won't conjure a husband that way."

The table falls uncomfortably silent. Elizabeth shoots me a sympathetic glance, but does not speak. No one does.

"I was merely admiring Edmund's resemblance to Victoria," I murmur, passing the salt cellar.

Father harrumphs. "Five seasons, Eleanor. Five. Your sisters were both married by their second."

"Not everyone can be as fortunate as Victoria and Elizabeth," Mother interjects gently.

"Fortunate?" Father's eyebrows rise so high they nearly disappear beneath his silver hairline. "Beauty makes its own fortune in the marriage mart. Eleanor simply wasn't blessed in that department. Plain as porridge, but there's no shame in admitting it."

I study the intricate pattern on my dinner plate, tracing the blue willow design with my eyes as heat rises to my cheeks. The worst part is not that Father speaks this way—he has always been blunt to the point of cruelty—but that he speaks the truth. I *am* plain. Unremarkable. Invisible.

"Father, really," Elizabeth protests, but her voice lacks conviction.

"What? The girl is three-and-twenty. Time she accepted reality instead of harboring false hopes. Might have had a chance with that second son of Lord Bexley two seasons ago, but even he found greener pastures."

The memory of Mr. Bexley's initial interest—and subsequent abandonment when the beautiful Miss Winters arrived in London—sends a fresh wave of humiliation through me. I had thought... but it doesn't matter what I thought.

I take a small sip of wine, willing my hand not to tremble. The footmen hover near the walls, pretending not to hear, but I know the servants' hall will buzz with fresh gossip about poor, plain Lady Eleanor later tonight.

Elizabeth's husband, Lord Devonham, clears his throat. "I hear Lady Cheddelton's ball was quite the crush last week. Were you in attendance, Lady Eleanor?"

I smile gratefully at him for the change of subject. "Yes. It was lovely."

What I don't say is how I spent most of the evening seated against the wall with the chaperones and dowagers, watching other young women dance. How I waited through three sets without a partner before Mother mercifully suggested we make an early departure.

Victoria bounces Edmund higher on her knee. "We miss so much of the Season now, being in the country with the children most of the year. But I wouldn't trade it for all the balls in London."

She gazes at her husband again with such naked adoration that my throat tightens. *Will anyone ever look at me that way? I think not.* My future stretches before me—a long, empty corridor of days spent as a maiden aunt, playing with my sisters' children, eventually becoming a companion to Mother in her old age. It's not a terrible fate. Many women live thus. *But oh, how I wish...*

I wish for arms to hold me. For children of my own. For someone who might value what little I have to offer. In my most secret heart, I long for a love like the ones I see before me, though I would never admit such foolishness aloud.

At least I have my music. At the pianoforte, I am transformed. My fingers speak what my lips cannot. The melodies that pour from my soul make me feel, for a few precious moments, that I am something more than plain, forgettable Eleanor.

After dinner, we withdraw to the drawing room, the gentlemen following shortly with their brandies. Elizabeth settles beside me on the small settee.

"Will you play for us, Eleanor? No one interprets Beethoven quite like you do."

I recognize the request for what it is—part kindness, part pity. My sister is offering me the one spotlight in which I don't fade to insignificance. Still, I nod and rise, smoothing my pale blue gown.

"Of course."

As I take my seat at the pianoforte, I feel the familiar calm descend. Here, at least, I know my worth. Here, my plainness doesn't matter. I place my fingers on the cool ivory keys and close my eyes briefly. When I begin to play, the drawing room, my father's criticisms, my hopeless future—all fade away. There is only the music, and for these few minutes, it is enough.

The final chord hangs in the air, then dissipates into silence. I remain still for a moment, fingertips lingering on the keys, reluctant to break the spell. Music is the only magic I possess in this world—the only time I feel truly seen, even if no eyes are upon me.

"Sublime, Eleanor," Elizabeth says, the first to break the reverent quiet that has settled over the drawing room. "Absolutely sublime."

I smile faintly as I close the pianoforte and rise. "Thank you."

Mother dabs at the corner of her eye with a lace handkerchief. "You play with such feeling, my dear."

"If only feeling translated to marriage prospects," Father mutters, draining his brandy.

I pretend not to hear as I reclaim my seat, grateful when the footmen enter with the tea service and an assortment of desserts. Victoria passes little Edmund to her husband and takes charge of the tea tray, a role she has assumed since her marriage, despite being my older sister.

"Sugar, Eleanor?" she asks, the silver tongs poised.

"Just one, please."

The familiar ritual of passing cups and selecting treats fills several minutes with pleasant mundanity. I choose a small marzipan confection, nibbling it slowly while Victoria regales us with tales of her eldest daughter's latest accomplishments.

"Amelia recited an entire poem from memory yesterday," she says proudly. "Four years old and already so clever."

"She takes after her mother," Lord Devonham says, his eyes warm with affection.

Victoria sets her teacup down with a delicate clink against its saucer. "Speaking of social engagements, I understand the Carrington Ball is tomorrow evening. Will you be attending, Eleanor?"

The question, though innocently posed, sends a ripple of tension through me. The Carrington Ball—one of the season's most anticipated events, where the fashionable elite will parade in their finest while scrutinizing everyone else with equal fervor. I resist the urge to touch my plain muslin gown, knowing all too well how it would pale beside the silks and satins that will adorn the ballroom tomorrow night.

"I had not quite decided," I reply, my fingers curling slightly around my teacup. "Father mentioned it, of course, but..."

Victoria blushes prettily, then sets down her cup with a decisive clink. "Oh! I nearly forgot to mention—we've received an invitation to Lady Harsgrove's ball a fortnight hence. Her son has returned from the Continent, and rumor has it she's determined to see him settled this Season."

"I recall meeting young Lord Harsgrove at Almack's some years ago," Elizabeth muses. "Decent dancer, if rather serious."

"You should accompany us, Eleanor," Victoria says suddenly, turning to me. "As our guest, of course."

I nearly choke on my tea. "Pardon?"

"Lady Harsgrove's ball. You must come with us," Victoria repeats, as if it's already decided. "I hear there will be several eligible bachelors in attendance besides Lord Harsgrove. Sir William Blackwood has recently inherited his uncle's fortune, and Mr. Penrose—you remember him, surely—has just returned from India quite well-established."

Elizabeth's teacup freezes halfway to her lips. "Victoria, I don't think that would be a good idea."

"Why ever not?" Victoria looks genuinely confused.

"Because..." Elizabeth hesitates, glancing at me apologetically. "Well, you know how these grand affairs can be. Lady Harsgrove is notoriously selective with her guest list. Throwing Eleanor into such a gathering might be... uncomfortable."

"For whom?" Victoria retorts, her cheeks flushing. "Are you suggesting our sister isn't good enough for Lady Harsgrove's drawing room?"

"Of course not," Elizabeth hisses, leaning forward. "I'm thinking of Eleanor's comfort. These ruthless marriage-minded mamas with their daughters in tow—you know how they can be. The cutting remarks, the pitying glances."

"I am still in the room," I remind them quietly, but neither sister seems to hear.

"She's three-and-twenty, not a green girl fresh from the schoolroom," Victoria argues. "And how is she to meet anyone suitable if we don't include her?"

"By throwing her to the wolves at one of the Season's most anticipated events? That's your solution?"

"Ladies," Mother interjects weakly, but Victoria has already drawn herself up, her eyes flashing.

"I have made up my mind. Eleanor will come with us, and that is final. The Devonhams and Halfords command enough consequence to ensure she is treated respectfully. And who knows? Perhaps without the pressure of an official Season, she might actually enjoy herself. Make a match, even."

Elizabeth sighs dramatically. "All I'm saying is—"

"I know precisely what you're saying, and I disagree," Victoria interrupts. "Eleanor deserves the same opportunities we had. It's not her fault that—"

I rise abruptly, unable to bear another moment of this discussion about my prospects—or lack thereof—as if I were not present. "Excuse me," I murmur, though I doubt either of them notices my departure.

I cross to the far window, drawing back the heavy velvet curtain. Outside, a dense fog has rolled in from the moors, obscuring everything beyond the formal garden. The world beyond Ravensbrook has disappeared into the mist, much as my hopes for a life of my own have slowly dissolved over the years.

How many times have I endured this same conversation? How many well-meaning attempts at matchmaking have ended in humiliation? My sisters, beautiful and happily married, cannot comprehend what it means to be overlooked, to be the woman whose name gentlemen forget, whose presence leaves no impression.

The fog presses against the glass like a living thing, and I place my palm against the cool pane, feeling the chill seep into my skin. It's no use. No amount of orchestrated introductions or strategic placements beside eligible gentlemen will change what I am—what I am not.

This is my destiny: to remain at Ravensbrook, to become Mother's companion as her health continues to decline, to be the spinster aunt who plays the pianoforte at family gatherings. I will watch my nieces and nephews grow, perhaps guide them through their own Seasons someday.

I will never know what it means to be chosen, to be cherished. I will never feel a lover's touch or hold a child of my own. The music that flows from my fingers will be my only legacy, notes that vanish into silence almost as soon as they're born.

I will never find love.

Behind me, my sisters continue their argument, their voices rising and falling like discordant notes in an otherwise empty composition. I remain at the window, a shadow against the glass, as insubstantial as the fog that blots out the world beyond.

I drift away from my sisters' bickering, moving from window to window like a ghost haunting its own halls, until their voices fade to a distant hum. Through the fog-shrouded glass, my reflection stares back at me - a pale, unremarkable thing with features that seem to blur and fade like watercolors left in the rain. My dark hair lies flat and lifeless against my temples, my hazel eyes appear dull in this grey light. Even my skin seems to merge with the mist beyond the window, as if nature itself conspires to render me invisible.

I trace a finger along my reflection, following the utterly ordinary line of my jaw, the uninspiring curve of my cheek. *What man would ever look at such a face with desire? What gentleman would gaze upon these features and find himself moved to poetry or passion?* No, I am meant for practical things - managing a household, preserving reputation, producing heirs. Love, that most precious of life's gifts, was never meant for one such as I.

I sigh deeply, pulling myself away from my melancholy reflections in the window. The fog beyond the glass has thickened, as impenetrable as my future seems to be. With reluctant steps, I make my way back toward the heated debate my sisters continue to wage on my behalf. It's both touching and mortifying how they argue over my prospects—or lack thereof—as if I were some chess piece to be strategically positioned rather than a woman of three-and-twenty with thoughts of my own.

"—must consider that she hasn't the confidence to withstand such scrutiny," Elizabeth is saying as I approach, her voice lowered but perfectly audible.

"And how is she to gain confidence locked away at Ravensbrook?" Victoria counters, bouncing Edmund with more vigor than the now-fussing child appreciates. "Really, Elizabeth, sometimes I think you—"

"I'm perfectly capable of deciding for myself," I interject softly as I reclaim my seat. Both sisters turn to me with identical expressions of surprise, as if they'd forgotten I could speak.

"Of course you are, darling," Victoria says quickly. "We were merely discussing—"

"My hopeless matrimonial prospects. Yes, I gathered as much." I smooth my skirts, arranging the pale blue fabric with careful attention. "I appreciate your concern, both of you, but perhaps we might discuss something else? The weather, perhaps? Or Lady Canwick's latest scandal?"

Father snorts from his armchair. "Weather and scandal—that's all you women ever talk about. No wonder Eleanor can't secure a husband, with such vapid conversation."

Mother shoots Father a quelling look before turning to me. "Eleanor, dear, I've been thinking. Perhaps we might visit Madame Roux in York this week? She's just received shipments of the most exquisite French silks, despite the blockade. A new gown might be just the thing to lift your spirits."

I stare at my mother, momentarily speechless. A new gown—as if silk and lace could somehow transform me into something I am not. As if the right shade of muslin might suddenly render me desirable, worthy of love.

"A capital idea," Elizabeth chimes in, clearly relieved by the change of subject. "I've heard that emerald green is quite the fashion this season. With your complexion, Eleanor—"

"With my complexion, I look sallow in green," I finish for her. "As you well know, having advised me against purchasing a green spencer just last spring."

"Perhaps a deep blue, then," Victoria suggests, shifting Edmund to her other knee. "To bring out the flecks of color in your eyes."

"Or rose," Mother adds hopefully. "To add a touch of warmth to your cheeks."

I feel something inside me twist painfully. They mean well—they all do—but their suggestions only underscore what we all know: that I require artifice and enhancement, that my natural state is insufficient. Plain Eleanor, who needs colored fabric to render her noticeable, who requires strategic placement at balls to secure even the most reluctant dance partners.

"That's very kind," I manage, keeping my voice steady. "But I don't believe a new dress will make much difference."

I glance around the drawing room, at my beautiful sisters with their handsome husbands, at my parents who still—despite everything—harbor hope that I will someday make a match worthy of the family name. I see the pity in their eyes, the well-intentioned concern, and I cannot bear it.

"Nothing will," I add softly, the words escaping before I can reconsider.

The silence that follows feels like a physical presence, heavy and suffocating. Mother's hand flutters to her throat, a gesture of distress she's employed since I was a child. Father shifts uncomfortably in his seat, suddenly finding great interest in the pattern of the carpet. My sisters exchange a look I can't quite interpret—part concern, part exasperation, perhaps?

"Eleanor," Elizabeth begins, her voice gentle. "You mustn't take such a dim view—"

"Why not?" The question emerges sharper than I intended. "Is it not better to accept reality than to continue nurturing false hopes? Is that not what Father himself advised not an hour ago at dinner?"

Father clears his throat. "Well, now, I didn't mean—"

"You meant precisely what you said," I counter, surprising myself with my boldness. "And you were right. I am plain. Unremarkable. Forgettable. Five Seasons have proven that beyond any doubt. No amount of French silk or strategic introductions will change that fundamental truth."

The silence returns, more profound than before. I feel lightheaded, dizzy with my own audacity. Never have I spoken so bluntly, so honestly about my situation. The relief of finally acknowledging what everyone in this room already knows is strangely liberating.

"Perhaps," I continue, more gently now, "it would be kinder to allow me to find peace with my circumstances rather than continuing this charade of hope."

Mother's eyes shine with unshed tears. "But my dear—"

"A new dress will not make me beautiful," I say with finality. "It will not make gentlemen see me when I have been invisible these five years past. It will not conjure a love match from thin air."

I rise from my seat, suddenly desperate for the solitude of my chambers, for the comfort of my pianoforte where I can pour these feelings into music rather than words.

"If you'll excuse me, I believe I shall retire. It's been a rather long evening."

Without waiting for a response, I curtsey and quit the room, maintaining my composure until I reach the grand staircase. Only then do I allow my carefully constructed façade to crumble, a single tear tracking down my cheek as I ascend toward the solitary refuge of my bedchamber.

Some truths, once spoken, cannot be reclaimed—and tonight, I have finally voiced the one truth I have spent years pretending not to know: that for women like me, some dreams remain forever beyond reach.

CHAPTER TWO
A MEDDLING SISTER
THE DUKE OF WESTMORELAND

I ride toward Waltham Manor, winter's breath biting at my cheeks despite the afternoon sun. My horse's hooves thunder against the frozen ground, the sound somehow matching the persistent rhythm of thoughts I cannot seem to outrun. The sprawling stone edifice of my ancestral home emerges from between the ancient oaks that have guarded it for centuries. Fifteen generations of Hanburies have lived and died within these walls. And I, the sixteenth Duke of Westmoreland, return to the same emptiness I left behind three days ago.

The grooms rush forward as I dismount in the courtyard, their movements efficient from years of practice. I nod curtly at their greetings. My boots echo against the polished marble of the entrance hall as I shrug off my greatcoat, handing it to Simmons, who has served as butler since before I was born.

"Your sister arrived an hour ago, Your Grace," he informs me, his face betraying no emotion beyond proper deference. "Lady

Anne requested that you join the family in the blue drawing room when you return."

I suppress a sigh. "Thank you, Simmons. I shall go up directly."

The familiar weight of duty settles upon my shoulders as I climb the grand staircase. Anne visits rarely enough from her estate in Derbyshire that I cannot reasonably avoid her company, though I suspect I know precisely what conversation awaits me. She has maintained a determined campaign regarding my marital status these past two seasons.

I pause at the doorway of the blue drawing room, taking in the scene before announcing my presence. Anne sits regally by the fireplace, her dark hair—so like my own—now threaded with silver at the temples. Her three daughters cluster around her, the youngest engaged with a book, the elder two whispering conspiratorially. My brother-in-law, Lord Blackwood, stands by the window, his lanky frame silhouetted against the fading light.

"Uncle Sebastian!" My eldest niece, Catherine, spots me first. At sixteen, she grows more like her mother daily, possessing the same forthright manner that makes Anne such a formidable presence.

"The prodigal duke returns," Henry Blackwood turns with a grin, crossing the room to clasp my hand warmly. "We were beginning to wonder if you'd abandoned us for more interesting company."

"I was merely seeing to business in York," I reply, though the explanation feels hollow even to my ears. The truth—that I had fled my own home to avoid precisely this gathering—remains unspoken.

"Business that couldn't wait until after your family's visit?" Anne's eyebrow arches in that particular way that makes me feel ten years old again, caught stealing tarts from the kitchen.

"Some matters require immediate attention," I counter, taking a seat across from her.

Dinner passes pleasantly enough, with my nieces providing most of the conversation. Young Sophie recounts her latest scholarly achievements with surprising eloquence for a child of twelve, while Margaret, the middle daughter at fourteen, speaks enthusiastically about her watercolors. I find myself relaxing slightly, lulled by the simple joy of family connection.

Until Anne strikes.

"I've heard Lady Cranwell's daughter made quite an impression at the Fairchild ball last week," she remarks, her tone deceptively casual as the footmen clear away the final course.

"Did she?" I maintain an air of disinterest, though I know precisely where this leads.

"Indeed. They say she plays the pianoforte beautifully and has had three offers already, despite this being her first season."

Henry catches my eye from across the table, his expression sympathetic. He has weathered seventeen years of marriage to my sister; he knows her tactical approaches.

"How fortunate for Lady Cranwell," I respond, reaching for my wine.

Anne continues undeterred. "The Harrington girl is said to be equally accomplished, though perhaps not quite as handsome. Still, her dowry is substantial, and her connections—"

"Anne." My voice cuts sharper than intended. "I appreciate your concern, but I have no interest in the discussion of debutantes."

The memory rises unbidden—Seraphina's face, beautiful and cold, as she returned my ring. "You understand, of course," she had said, her voice never wavering. "Lord Easton's offer is simply more advantageous." Three years have passed, yet the humiliation burns fresh whenever I allow myself to remember.

"Sebastian." Anne's voice softens. "You cannot allow one woman's poor judgment to determine the course of your life. It has been three years."

"A fact of which I am perfectly aware." The chill in my voice could freeze the Thames in August.

"And you are equally aware, I presume, that should you fail to produce an heir, Waltham will pass to Cousin Edmund upon your death?"

The mention of our dissolute cousin—a gambler and libertine whose debts are as notorious as his indiscretions—provokes exactly the response Anne intends. A tightness grips my chest. The thought of Edmund Hanbury presiding over the estate our father preserved through careful stewardship is intolerable.

"Girls," Henry intervenes smoothly, "perhaps you might retire to the music room? I believe your uncle had the pianoforte tuned last week."

The girls need no further encouragement, filing out with curtseyed farewells. I rise the moment they depart.

"Anne, if you'll excuse me—"

"Sebastian, I speak only out of concern—"

"Henry," I interrupt, "might I interest you in a brandy? I acquired an excellent cask from France last month."

Henry, bless him, recognizes the escape for what it is. "I would be delighted."

Anne's disapproving gaze follows us as we retreat to my study, where I immediately pour two generous measures of amber liquid. The first sip burns satisfyingly down my throat.

"She means well," Henry offers, settling into a leather chair as I strike a match to light a cigar.

"She means to manage my life as she did when we were children," I counter, though without true heat. "I am eight and twenty, not eight."

"And she is your only family," he reminds me gently. "After your parents..." He trails off, knowing the wound remains tender despite the decade that has passed since fever took them both within a fortnight of each other.

I exhale a plume of smoke toward the ceiling. "What would you have me do? Parade through London ballrooms examining girls half my age like prize mares at Tattersall's?"

"God forbid," Henry laughs. "Though I must admit, this season offers some promising candidates. Lady Winchester's eldest has both wit and fortune, they say. And the Duke of Ashford's ward—though perhaps a bit serious for your taste."

"And which of these paragons of womanhood would you recommend I saddle myself with for eternity?" The brandy loosens my tongue, allowing the bitterness to seep through.

Henry studies me thoughtfully. "You know, marriage need not be a prison sentence. Some of us find it rather agreeable."

"Some of us were fortunate enough to find wives with more than ambition beneath their beautiful exteriors," I retort.

I swirl the brandy in my glass, watching the amber liquid catch the firelight. "The only reason to marry now would be to secure the succession. Nothing more."

"A noble goal," Henry drawls with an exaggerated bow from his chair. "God save Waltham Manor from Cousin Edmund's clutches."

Despite my foul mood, I feel my lips twitch. Henry has always possessed the frustrating ability to pierce through my darker humors.

"Though it needn't be a London debutante," he continues, settling deeper into his chair. "Lady Fairhaven's second daughter is said to be uncommonly sensible, and they winter at their country estate not fifteen miles from here. Convenient, wouldn't you say?"

"Ah, yes, the practical approach to matrimony. Tell me, is that how you wooed my sister? 'Uncommonly sensible and conveniently located?'"

Henry feigns offense, placing a hand over his heart. "I'll have you know I was positively smitten with Anne's sensible nature. The way she organized the linen cupboards quite took my breath away."

I cannot help but laugh. "A romantic for the ages."

"Not to mention Lady Thornfield's niece," Henry continues, undeterred. "The family has taken a house near the village for the winter. I believe she plays the harp. Imagine the pastoral bliss—your brooding silences accompanied by angelic strumming."

"Heavenly," I deadpan. "Though I suspect the young lady might take exception to my less angelic habits."

Henry raises an eyebrow. "Such as?"

"My preference for brandy over tea, cigars over conversation, and solitude over social gatherings."

"Trifling matters," Henry waves dismissively. "What woman wouldn't overlook such minor foibles for a duke with your... abundant charms?"

"My abundant fortune, you mean."

"I was attempting delicacy, but yes, precisely that." Henry grins over his glass. "Though I did hear Lady Merriweather's daughter has refused two viscounts already this season. Perhaps she's holding out for a duke with a notorious scowl and sparkling personality."

I snort into my brandy. "Does she also enjoy long, silent rides through rain-soaked moors and dinners without conversation?"

"One can but hope." Henry's eyes twinkle with mischief. "Though perhaps you'd prefer the widow Carrington? At least there you'd face no disappointment on your wedding night."

"Henry!" I exclaim, nearly choking on my drink. "That is my future duchess you're speaking of."

"Ah, so you admit you're in the market."

"For a horse, perhaps. Not a wife."

The familiar rhythm of our banter soothes something in me. Henry has been more brother than in-law these past ten years, one of the few people in whose company I can simply exist without pretense.

"Enough about matrimonial prospects," I declare, setting down my glass with finality. "Did you hear about my recent windfall at White's? I relieved Lord Pemberton of five thousand pounds at whist last Tuesday."

Henry whistles. "Good God. Anne will have my head if I sit at cards with you again. Did Pemberton take it well?"

"As well as one might expect." I cannot help the satisfied smile that spreads across my face. "Though he was considerably more distressed when I won his prized Arabian in the next hand."

"You didn't."

"I most certainly did. A magnificent creature—seventeen hands, black as midnight with a temperament to match. Pemberton has been showing him off all season, claiming he's descended from the Sultan of Morocco's personal stables."

"And is he?"

I shrug. "Who can say? But he's the finest piece of horseflesh I've seen in years. You must come to the stables tomorrow."

"Pemberton must have been foxed to wager such an animal."

"Spectacularly so," I agree, refilling our glasses. "Though his face when I called his bluff..." I shake my head, remembering the man's slack-jawed shock. "Worth every penny."

The study door bursts open, interrupting our laughter. Anne's middle daughter, Margaret, stands breathless in the doorway, her face pale.

"Papa! Sophie's fallen on the stairs—her ankle!"

Henry is on his feet instantly. "Where is she?"

"The front hall. Mama sent me to fetch you."

He sets down his glass and strides toward the door, pausing only briefly to catch my eye. "We'll continue this tomorrow. I want to see this miraculous horse."

"Of course," I nod, rising as well. "Can I be of assistance?"

"No need," he calls back, already following Margaret down the corridor. "Likely just a sprain. Anne will have her wrapped and fussing in bed within the hour."

The door closes behind them, leaving me alone with the crackling fire and half-empty decanter. The sudden silence feels oppressive after the warmth of our conversation. I wander to the window, pulling back the heavy curtain to gaze outside.

A dense fog has settled over the grounds, transforming the familiar landscape into something ghostly and indistinct. The great oaks that line the drive are mere shadows, their branches reaching like spectral fingers into the night. I press my hand against the cold glass, watching my breath create a circle of condensation.

Five thousand pounds and a prized Arabian. A triumph by any measure—yet the victory feels hollow standing here alone. The manor houses thirty-eight rooms, most of them empty save for furniture and memories. The portraits of my ancestors line the walls, their painted eyes following me with silent judgment. Sixteen generations of Hanburys, and I may be the last.

I turn from the window, my reflection fragmenting in the glass. The brandy has lost its savor, the fire its warmth. For all my wealth, my title, my carefully cultivated independence—what remains at the end of each day? This emptiness that no amount of cards or horses or brandy can fill.

This vast house echoes with silence. Perhaps the true gamble is not at the card table but in life itself—the wager of one's solitude against the possibility of something more. I wonder, not for the first time, if this disconnection is all that remains for me, or if somewhere, somehow, there exists a completion I have yet to find.

CHAPTER THREE
THE CARRINGTON BALL
LADY ELEANOR HARTWOOD

The Carrington Ball glitters like the night sky above us. Crystal chandeliers drip with candlelight, casting golden pools across the polished floor where couples twirl in perfect rhythm. I stand at the periphery—my usual position—watching the spectacle unfold with a peculiar mixture of detachment and wistfulness.

"Eleanor, do stop lurking by the punch bowl." Victoria materializes beside me, her crimson gown a stark contrast to my muted blue one. "I have someone I should like you to meet."

I suppress a sigh. These introductions follow a tediously predictable pattern. Victoria, ever hopeful despite five fruitless Seasons of attempting to secure me a match, will present me to some gentleman. He will bow politely, make perfunctory conversation while his eyes scan the room for more appealing prospects, and then excuse himself at the earliest opportunity.

"Lord Rothwell," Victoria says, her voice pitched to its most charming register, "may I present my sister, Lady Eleanor Hartwood?"

The gentleman is tall with pleasant enough features. His eyes flicker to me, then away, then reluctantly back. "A pleasure, Lady Eleanor."

I curtsy. "The pleasure is mine, my lord."

His gaze darts beyond my shoulder almost immediately. I recognize the look—searching for escape.

"My sister is quite accomplished at the pianoforte," Victoria adds desperately.

"Indeed?" Lord Rothwell shifts his weight. "How delightful. I am afraid I know little of music myself. Lady Eleanor, if you will excuse me, I believe I see an acquaintance I must greet."

He is gone before I can even nod. Victoria's smile tightens imperceptibly.

"He seemed in rather a hurry," I murmur.

Victoria smooths an invisible wrinkle on her glove. "He is simply overwhelmed by the crush of people. Come, I believe Lord Hathaway's second son is by the windows."

And so it continues. Three more introductions, three more polite retreats. I begin to feel like a piece of furniture that has been mistakenly placed in the ballroom—acknowledged briefly, then forgotten.

After Victoria's attention is claimed by the Countess of Whitley, I retreat to the edge of the dance floor. The orchestra strikes up a lively country dance. I watch as gentlemen approach young ladies, extending hands and invitations. Two gentlemen walk in my direction, and I feel a ridiculous flutter of hope. They pass me without a glance, continuing to a pair of giggling debutantes.

Couples form on the dance floor—handsome men with beautiful women, each complementing the other like perfectly matched bookends. The gentleman leads, strong and confident; the lady follows, graceful and poised. They move together as if created for this purpose, to orbit one another in the codified steps of the dance, smiling into each other's eyes.

I will never know what that feels like.

A tall gentleman with golden hair pauses near me, and for one disorienting moment, our eyes meet. He smiles—not at me, I realize with a familiar sinking feeling, but at someone behind me. A moment later, he bows to a lovely young woman in pale green silk who accepts his hand with a radiant smile.

The ballroom suddenly feels too warm, too crowded. The music, which I normally love, scrapes against my nerves like a bow drawn incorrectly across violin strings. I need air.

I slip through the French doors that lead to the garden, careful not to draw attention to my departure. The night air washes over me, cool and sweet with the scent of roses. I walk along the gravel path, away from the light and music.

The garden is deserted, everyone drawn to the spectacle inside. Above me, stars puncture the velvet darkness, countless and brilliant. I tilt my head back, breathing deeply.

At home, I might sit at my pianoforte now, letting the music speak what I cannot.

"Here you are."

I start, turning to find Victoria standing at the edge of the path, her silhouette outlined by the light from the house.

"Victoria. I was merely getting some air."

She comes closer, the rustle of her gown against the gravel unnaturally loud in the quiet garden. "You always disappear. At every ball, every dinner, every gathering. Why do you do this to yourself, Eleanor?"

"Do what?"

"Hide away. Refuse to try. How do you expect to make connections when you vanish the moment conversation becomes difficult?"

"I do not hide," I protest weakly.

Victoria gives me a look of sisterly exasperation. "Then what would you call this excursion to the darkest corner of the garden?"

I turn away, studying the pattern of stars overhead rather than meet her gaze. "I am merely being practical. Why should I torture myself with false hopes? I am three and twenty, Victoria. If I were to make a match, it would have happened by now."

"Eleanor—"

"No," I interrupt, surprising myself with my vehemence. "I have accepted my future. I shall be Aunt Eleanor to your children and Elizabeth's, and I shall be content with my music. It is better this way—I will never marry, so why meet anyone? Why subject myself to these humiliations?"

The truth of my words settles over me with surprising peace. I have known this for years, really. I am not as beautiful as my sisters. I do not sparkle in conversation. I am... forgettable. Unremarkable. And that is all right. Not everyone can be extraordinary.

Victoria pulls her shawl tighter around her shoulders, giving me a look of mingled pity and exasperation. "Do not stay out here too long, Eleanor. The night air grows chill, and you know how susceptible you are to colds." Her tone softens. "I only want to see you happy, you know."

"I know," I murmur, though in truth, I wonder if she truly understands what would make me happy. Not these endless balls and uncomfortable introductions, certainly.

"Think on what I said." She touches my arm briefly. "And do come inside before you catch your death."

I nod, not trusting my voice. Victoria lingers a moment longer, then turns and makes her way back along the gravel path, her crimson gown catching the light from the ballroom as she moves.

I watch as she ascends the three shallow steps to the terrace. Lord Devonham—her husband—appears in the doorway as if summoned by some sixth sense that his wife approaches. He extends his hand, and Victoria takes it with the casual confidence of a woman who has never doubted her place in the world. He bends to whisper something in her ear, and she laughs—a bright, lovely sound that carries across the garden.

My sister's happiness should warm me. Instead, I feel the chill Victoria warned me about, though it comes from within rather than from the night air.

Lord Devonham leads Victoria back into the ballroom, and through the tall windows, I watch as they join the dance. My sister moves with the easy grace she has possessed since childhood. Her husband gazes at her with unmistakable adoration. Ten years of marriage, and still he looks at her as though she hangs the moon.

I drift closer to the windows, drawn by the light and music despite myself. The ball continues unabated, a kaleidoscope of color and movement. No one glances toward the garden; no one notices my absence. If I were to walk away now, to return to Ravensbrook Hall and take to my bed, would anyone even remark upon it before the carriage was called at the evening's end?

I know the answer, and there is a curious freedom in it. I am unobserved. Invisible. I could stand here all night, watching life unfold beyond the glass, and remain undisturbed.

A stir at the ballroom entrance draws my attention. Three gentlemen have arrived—fashionably late, of course. The collective awareness of the room shifts, like flowers turning toward the sun. I see ladies adjusting their posture, touching their hair, and exchanging meaningful glances with one another.

I understand their reaction when I catch sight of the tallest of the three men. Even from this distance, I can discern that he is uncommonly handsome—broad-shouldered beneath his impeccably tailored evening coat, with dark hair that gleams in the candlelight. He moves with the easy confidence of a man accustomed to commanding attention, acknowledging greetings with a slight inclination of his head as he and his companions make their way across the ballroom.

"The Duke of Westmoreland," I whisper to myself, recognizing him now. I have seen him from afar at other events, though we have never been introduced. *Why would we be?* He is considered one of London's most eligible bachelors—wealthy, titled, and devastatingly attractive. I am... well, I am standing alone in a garden while life happens elsewhere.

He pauses at the edge of the dance floor, surveying the room with a cool detachment that somehow only enhances his appeal. Then his gaze settles on a young woman in a gown of pale gold—Miss Winters, if I recall correctly, this Season's most celebrated beauty. He approaches her, bows, and extends his hand. Even from here, I can see the flush of pleasure on her cheeks as she accepts.

They take their places as the orchestra begins a waltz. I press closer to the window, my breath creating a small cloud on the glass. The Duke of Westmoreland and Miss Winters move together in perfect harmony, his hand at the proper position on her waist, her fingers resting lightly on his shoulder. They are a striking pair—she fair and delicate, he dark and commanding.

Most notable, however, is the way he looks at her. His expression is one of complete focus, as though she is the only person in the crowded ballroom. His eyes never leave her face as they turn about the floor, and when she speaks, a smile touches his lips—transforming his austere features into something warm and approachable.

I have danced, of course. Dutiful gentlemen have led me through quadrilles and country dances at the insistence of their mothers or my own family. But no man has ever looked at me the way the Duke now gazes at Miss Winters—as though memorizing every detail of her face, as though her words are precious gems to be collected and treasured.

What must it feel like to be the center of such attention? To know that, in that moment, you are the most important person in his world? I press my hand against the cool glass, separated from that glittering scene by more than just a pane of window.

The waltz continues, and I remain where I am, a silent observer to a pleasure I will never know. The Duke says something that makes Miss Winters laugh, her head tipping back to reveal the elegant line of her throat. His smile deepens in response, revealing a dimple in his left cheek. The intimacy of that shared moment makes me feel even more the intruder, though neither of them knows I watch.

I sigh as the Duke of Westmoreland and Miss Winters disappear around the corner of the ballroom, swallowed by the crush of elegant bodies. My entertainment for the evening has vanished like morning mist under a summer sun. How peculiar that watching strangers dance should provide such bitter solace, yet here I stand, bereft at their departure.

The night air no longer feels refreshing but merely cold against my skin. The distant strains of the orchestra beckon me back inside—not because I might participate in their merriment, but because standing alone in a darkened garden has become suddenly unbearable. At least within the ballroom, I might pretend to be part of the glittering tableau.

I smooth down my unremarkable blue gown and pinch a hint of color into my cheeks before slipping back through the French doors. No one notices my return. *Why should they?* Lady Eleanor Hartwood, moving from one shadow to another, as substantial as a wisp of smoke.

My feet carry me directly to the refreshment table, where I claim a crystal goblet of punch. The sweet-tart liquid does little to wash away the taste of melancholy, but it gives my hands something to do. I reach for a small tartlet, then a bit of sugared fruit, eating without tasting. These little movements —reaching, sipping, dabbing at my lips with a napkin— provide the illusion of purpose.

"I assure you, Charlotte, it was dreadfully dull."

The voice cuts through the general hum of conversation, commanding attention by its volume alone. I glance up to find Miss Winters standing not three feet away, her golden gown catching the candlelight as she gestures emphatically to a friend. She has not noticed me—few ever do—but I find myself frozen in place, punch glass halfway to my lips.

"But he is *so* handsome," her companion protests, a petite brunette whose name escapes me. "And a Duke! Surely the waltz was pleasant at the very least?"

Miss Winters tosses her head, sending golden curls bouncing against her bare shoulders. "Handsome he may be, but the Duke of Westmoreland is as cold as a statue. All that time, and not a single word beyond the merest pleasantries! Just looking down his aristocratic nose at everyone as though we were insects to be cataloged."

I nearly choke on my punch. *Cold? The man I observed had seemed entirely captivated, his attention fixed upon Miss Winters with unmistakable warmth. Had I imagined that smile, that dimple, that look of complete absorption?*

"Perhaps he was simply nervous," suggests the brunette, lowering her voice slightly. "They say he has been rather... reserved since that business with Lady Seraphina."

Miss Winters sniffs. "Reserved is a charitable description. I tell you, Charlotte, I might as well have danced with a block of ice. And his conversation! *'You dance well, Miss Winters.' 'The orchestra plays tolerably tonight, do they not?'* As though he were reading from a manual of approved ballroom utterances."

I should move away. Eavesdropping is beneath even my limited dignity. Yet my feet remain rooted to the spot as Miss Winters continues her complaint.

"And to think Mama insisted I save him a dance! 'A duke, Georgiana,' she said. 'A duke with fifty thousand a year and three magnificent estates.' Well, he could have sixty thousand and a dozen palaces, and I should still find him insufferable."

Charlotte glances around nervously. "Georgiana, perhaps we should—"

"Oh, who cares if he hears me? Let him know that not every woman in London swoons at his approach. Imagine—such wealth and connections, such a face and figure—and he cannot turn a single interesting thought in his head nor speak a word that might capture one's attention!"

My mind reels at this assessment. *How can two people observe the same man and see such different qualities?* I had witnessed a gentleman utterly focused on his partner, smiling at her words, moving with natural grace. Miss Winters had experienced a cold automaton, barely present despite physical proximity.

"The worst of it," Miss Winters continues, leaning closer to her friend, "is that he seemed positively relieved when our dance concluded. Bowed and walked away without a backward glance! I tell you, Charlotte, I have never been so insulted."

"Perhaps he simply—"

"No, he is clearly incapable of proper feeling. I pity the woman who eventually becomes his duchess. She shall perish from boredom within a fortnight."

I place my empty punch glass on the table with a soft clink. The sound, insignificant as it is, draws Miss Winters' attention briefly to me. Her eyes pass over my face without recognition or interest before returning to her friend.

"Come, Charlotte, let us find Lord Beeston. At least he knows how to smile without looking as though his face might crack from the effort."

They move away in a rustle of silk and laughter, leaving me by the refreshment table with the curious feeling of having glimpsed behind a curtain I had not known was there. The Duke of Westmoreland—cold and disinterested according to the beautiful Miss Winters, yet seemingly attentive to my distant observation.

How fascinating that the same man could present such different aspects. Perhaps we all contain such contradictions—appearing one way to certain eyes and entirely different to others. Even I, plain Eleanor Hartwood, might seem different through varying perspectives. Though I doubt anyone has troubled themselves to look deeply enough to form any opinion of me beyond "unremarkable."

I find myself wondering which version of the Duke is true—the attentive partner I observed or the cold aristocrat Miss Winters described. Or perhaps, most likely of all, both are merely fragments of a whole person neither of us truly knows.

CHAPTER FOUR
THE HARSGROVE BALL
THE DUKE OF WESTMORELAND

I stand at the edge of Lady Harsgrove's ballroom, nursing a glass of champagne as I survey the scene before me. The chandelier casts a warm glow across the polished floor, illuminating a veritable sea of silk, satin, and scheming mothers. Not that I can blame them—apparently, I am the great matrimonial prize of the season. A fact I only learned upon our arrival, when no fewer than three matrons descended upon me with the fervor of hawks spotting a wounded rabbit.

The country estate's ballroom, though smaller than the grand London venues, has been transformed admirably for the occasion. Festoons of spring flowers—mostly lilacs and early roses—hang from every available surface, their sweet scent mixing with perfume, beeswax candles, and the inevitable hint of nervous perspiration that accompanies these affairs. Musicians play a lively quadrille, though the dancers seem distracted, their eyes constantly darting in my direction.

"Westmoreland!" Lady Harsgrove herself approaches, a plump woman with remarkably red cheeks and an unnerving ability to corner a man regardless of how deliberately he positions himself near an exit. "You must meet the Misses Langley. Such accomplished young ladies—both play the harp, you know."

"How delightful," I respond with practiced cordiality, though I cannot imagine a more tedious prospect than listening to amateur harpists. "Perhaps later, Lady Harsgrove. I've only just arrived."

She clucks disapprovingly but moves on to her next victim. I catch Anne's eye across the room. My dear sister smiles broadly, entirely too pleased with herself. When I raise an eyebrow in silent accusation, she merely shrugs and turns back to her conversation with Lady Mumford. I should have known something was amiss when Anne insisted we attend this provincial gathering. She has never before shown such enthusiasm for Lady Harsgrove's annual country ball.

I weave through the crowd toward my sister, dodging hopeful introductions with remarkable agility born of years of practice. When I reach Anne's side, I bend to whisper in her ear.

"You told them I am looking for a wife?"

Anne turns, the picture of innocence. "I may have mentioned you were considering matrimonial prospects."

"Considering? From the way these women are circling, one would think I had announced my intention to propose before midnight."

"Don't be dramatic, Sebastian. You need a wife, and every eligible young lady in three counties is here tonight." She pats my arm. "Think of it as efficiency."

"I will think of it as betrayal," I mutter, though without true rancor. Anne means well, even if her methods are questionable. "At least you could have warned me."

"Would you have come if I had?"

I have no answer for that, which is answer enough. Anne smiles triumphantly.

"There's Lady Fairhaven with her second daughter," Anne says, nodding toward a tall, distinguished woman shepherding a girl in pale blue. "Jane, I believe. Quite musical, they say."

Before I can protest, Anne waves to Lady Fairhaven, who immediately changes course like a battleship spotting an enemy vessel.

"Lady Anne!" Lady Fairhaven exclaims, her voice carrying across the crowded room. "And Your Grace! What a pleasure."

I bow slightly. "Lady Fairhaven."

"May I present my daughter, Lady Jane?"

The girl curtseys, her gaze firmly fixed on the floor. I cannot properly see her face, only the top of her head with its unfashionably simple arrangement of dark brown hair. She is neither strikingly beautiful nor particularly plain—simply unremarkable. The type of young lady who blends into the wallpaper at these affairs.

"Your Grace," she murmurs, her voice barely audible above the music.

Before I can offer more than a perfunctory greeting, I am ambushed from the left.

"Duke of Westmoreland! What a delightful surprise!" Lady Thornfield appears, clutching the arm of a young woman with flaming red hair and a determined expression. "Have you met my niece, Miss Phillips? Just arrived from Bath. Plays the pianoforte magnificently."

I nod politely, acutely aware that Lady Fairhaven and her daughter still stand before me, creating an awkward tableau.

"Your Grace!" Another voice joins the fray as Lady Merriweather approaches, daughter in tow. "How fortuitous! Amelia was just saying she hoped to see you this evening."

The girl—presumably Amelia—blushes furiously but manages a practiced smile that suggests she was indeed saying no such thing.

Within moments, I find myself surrounded by a semicircle of hopeful mothers and their increasingly uncomfortable daughters. Lady Fairhaven jostles for position, while Lady Thornfield recites her niece's accomplishments as though reading from a sales catalog. Lady Merriweather simply stands too close, the feathers from her turban occasionally brushing my cheek in a way that makes me want to sneeze.

The daughters themselves range from boldly flirtatious to mortified, but all wear the same underlying expression of evaluation, assessing my worth as a potential husband with the clinical precision of horse traders. I would find it amusing if it were not so damnably uncomfortable.

Over the heads of my admirers, I spot Henry—dear, reliable Henry—conversing with the local vicar. With a muttered excuse about fetching refreshments, I extract myself from the maternal gauntlet and make a direct line for my brother-in-law.

"Henry," I begin without preamble, taking him firmly by the arm and steering him toward a less populated corner, "I believe I might murder your wife before the evening concludes."

Henry's eyes twinkle with undisguised amusement. "Ah, I see the marriage market has opened for business." He glances toward the cluster of ladies now watching us intently. "Rather a healthy crop this year."

"This is no laughing matter," I hiss. "She has practically advertised me as ready for the slaughter. Did you know of this scheme?"

I regard Henry with suspicion as he raises his hands in mock surrender, his mouth twitching with poorly concealed mirth.

"Upon my honor, Sebastian, I knew nothing of Anne's matchmaking schemes. Though I must admit'—he glances over my shoulder at the gathering of eager mamas—" the spectacle is rather entertaining."

Despite my irritation, I find myself chuckling. Henry has that effect—his good humor is infectious even in the most trying circumstances. "I'm glad someone is enjoying the evening."

"Come now, it cannot be so terrible to have half the eligible young ladies in Yorkshire vying for your attention." He takes a sip of his wine. "Most men would consider it a blessing rather than a burden."

"Most men haven't had their engagement end in public humiliation," I mutter, the memory of Seraphina's betrayal still sharp despite the passing years.

Henry's expression sobers. "Fair point. But not all women are like Miss Ashworth."

Before I can respond, the musicians bring their current piece to a conclusion. After a brief pause filled with the rustle of fans and hushed conversations, they strike up the opening notes of a quadrille. The effect is immediate—like a complex dance itself, couples begin forming on the floor, gentlemen bowing to selected partners, young ladies curtsying in response.

And then, with an almost palpable weight, I feel dozens of hopeful gazes settle upon me.

From across the room, I spot Anne watching expectantly, clearly waiting to see which young lady will receive the honor of my first dance. Better to choose quickly and on my own terms than to have some determined mama thrust her daughter into my path.

I hesitate, scanning the room for the least objectionable option. Henry sighs dramatically beside me.

"For God's sake, man." With an unexpectedly firm push

between my shoulder blades, he propels me forward. "Choose someone before they start drawing lots."

Thrown off balance both literally and figuratively, I find myself drifting toward Lady Fairhaven and her daughter Jane, who stands with quiet dignity despite her mother's obvious matchmaking efforts. Something about her reserved manner appeals to me—at least she isn't giggling or batting her eyelashes in my direction.

"Lady Jane," I bow slightly, "would you do me the honor of this dance?"

She looks genuinely surprised, her dark eyes widening momentarily before she composes herself. "I would be delighted, Your Grace."

Taking her gloved hand, I lead her to the floor, aware of the disappointed sighs in our wake. As we take our positions, I notice Lady Fairhaven's triumphant expression as she turns to her neighbors, clearly savoring her daughter's selection for the first dance.

The quadrille begins, and Lady Jane proves to be a competent dancer—neither so accomplished as to appear showy nor so awkward as to require constant guidance. As we move through the patterns, I find my attention wandering to the other couples in the set.

Miss Phillips, with her vibrant red hair and determined expression, has secured Lord Humphrey as a partner. Her movements are precise and confident, perhaps too much so. Across from us, the ethereal blonde Miss Edgerton floats through the steps with a dreamy quality that suggests her mind is elsewhere. Beside her, Miss Thornbury laughs too loudly at something her partner says, her plump cheeks flushed with what might be genuine amusement or merely exertion.

Each young lady, I realize with some surprise, possesses her own particular charm. Even Lady Jane, with her quiet grace and unremarkable features, has a certain tranquility about her that stands out in this artificial setting.

"Are you finding the country air agreeable, Your Grace?" Lady Jane's soft voice interrupts my observations.

"Quite refreshing after London," I reply automatically, the polite response requiring no thought.

She nods, apparently satisfied with this minimal exchange, and we complete the remainder of the dance in companionable silence.

The quadrille ends, and I escort Lady Jane back to her mother. Before Lady Fairhaven can engage me in conversation, I am intercepted by Lady Merriweather, who practically thrusts her daughter Amelia into my path. Courtesy demands I request the next dance, and so begins my rotation through the ballroom's offerings.

Miss Amelia Merriweather proves to be a surprisingly witty conversationalist, though her tendency to step on my toes somewhat diminishes the pleasure of our interaction. For the third dance, I select Miss Thornbury, whose enthusiasm for the country dance leaves me slightly breathless. By the fourth set, with Miss Edgerton's vacant chatter buzzing in my ears, I feel as though I might suffocate from the combined effects of perfume, expectation, and unsubtle matrimonial hints.

"If you'll excuse me," I murmur as the music concludes, "I find I'm in need of some air."

Without waiting for a response, I make my escape, slipping through the French doors that lead to the veranda. The cool night air hits my face like a blessing, and I exhale deeply, loosening my cravat with one finger.

What is happening to me tonight? I've danced with a dozen eligible young women without the slightest difficulty, yet here I stand, unable to simply select one and be done with it. Why am I making this so unnecessarily complicated? Is it merely the abundance of choices that paralyzes me—like a man starving before a feast, suddenly unable to decide which morsel to taste first? Or perhaps it's that none of them stir anything beyond the most perfunctory interest. They blend together in my mind: a parade of silk gowns, practiced smiles, and carefully rehearsed accomplishments, each one indistinguishable from the last. After Seraphina, I swore I would approach marriage with cold practicality. Yet something in me still rebels against such a clinical selection, as though some stubborn, foolish part of my soul demands more than I have any right to expect.

The veranda is mercifully empty, lit only by the soft glow spilling from the ballroom windows and the silver light of a three-quarter moon. In the distance, the dark shapes of Lady Harsgrove's formal gardens stretch toward the woods at the edge of the property. The scent of roses mingles with the earthy dampness of approaching rain.

"This is precisely why I avoid these provincial affairs," I mutter to myself, leaning against the stone balustrade. The tension in my shoulders begins to ease as the sounds of the ball—the music, the laughter, the constant buzz of conversation—recede into the background.

Having regained my composure, I straighten and turn, intending to return to the ball before Anne sends out a search party. As I do, a movement in the shadows at the far end of the veranda catches my eye.

A figure stands there—a young woman, her face half-illuminated by moonlight, half-hidden in darkness. She appears as startled by my presence as I am by hers, clutching what appears to be a shawl more tightly around her shoulders.

"Do forgive me," I say, hastily composing myself and feeling rather foolish for having been caught muttering to myself like some half-mad creature. "I did not know anyone was here."

The young woman hesitates before stepping fully from the shadows into the silvery wash of moonlight. She is no beauty —not by society's exacting standards. Her features, while pleasant enough, lack the striking quality that turns heads in crowded ballrooms. Her dark hair is arranged simply, without the elaborate curls and ornaments favored by the season's celebrated beauties. Her gown, though well-made, is unremarkable in its modest cut and subdued color.

But her eyes... her eyes tell an entirely different story. Large and expressive, they seem to hold depths that her quiet demeanor attempts to conceal. There is an intelligence there, keen and observant, and something else—a vulnerability, perhaps, or a carefully guarded passion. They remind me, oddly enough, of still waters that run unfathomably deep. Those eyes observe me now with a mixture of wariness and curiosity that I find strangely compelling, despite my usual indifference to ladies who fail to meet society's superficial criteria for beauty.

I watch as she retreats, her modest gown disappearing into the crowd with neither flourish nor fanfare. There is something oddly disarming about the way she withdraws—not with the practiced coyness of a society beauty playing at hard-to-get, but with the genuine discomfort of someone who prefers to remain unnoticed.

Most ladies of my acquaintance would have lingered, offering some trivial remark to extend our conversation, perhaps a coquettish smile or a meaningful glance. The lady possesses none of these artifices. She simply... *leaves*, as if our conversation had reached its natural conclusion, requiring no elaborate social dance to extricate herself.

I find myself staring after her long after she has vanished among the glittering throng, wondering why her abrupt departure leaves me with this peculiar sensation of incompletion. It is most irregular, this feeling—almost as if I had been in the midst of deciphering a complex piece of music only to have the sheet snatched away before I could grasp its full melody.

CHAPTER FIVE
THE VERANDA
LADY ELEANOR HARTWOOD

I cannot believe what has just happened. The Duke of Westmoreland himself, standing not ten feet away on the same veranda where I had sought refuge from the overwhelming crush of the ballroom. I freeze, hoping my plain gray gown might render me as invisible as I usually am at these affairs. My heart hammers against my ribs like the staccato notes of Herr Beethoven's Fifth Symphony.

He hasn't noticed me. Thank heavens. I've heard the whispers about him over the Seasons—his wealth, his land, his impossibly high standards. And of course, the broken engagement that left him bitter and cold toward all women of marriageable age. And, just like the previous night, at the Carrington Ball, I can't help but stare at him from my shadowed corner. Even in profile, the Duke cuts a striking figure—tall and imposing in his perfectly tailored evening clothes, the severe black of his coat emphasizing the breadth of his shoulders. His features are aristocratic, almost severe:

the strong jaw, the high cheekbones, the proud nose. But it's his mouth that draws my attention—full lips pressed into a tight line of disapproval as he surveys the ballroom.

"This is precisely why I avoid these provincial affairs," he mutters to no one, his deep voice carrying just far enough for me to hear. The disdain in his tone makes me flinch.

I shift my weight, and the floorboard beneath me creaks traitorously. His head turns sharply, and suddenly those dark eyes—eyes I've heard described as "penetrating" in a dozen different drawing rooms—are fixed directly on mine. My breath catches in my throat. For one terrible moment, I feel utterly exposed, as though he can see straight through my unremarkable gray gown to the ridiculous, traitorous heart pounding beneath.

His brow furrows slightly, and I see his lips part as if to speak. Before he can utter a word, I gather my skirts and slip sideways into the crowd, moving as quickly as dignity allows. My cheeks burn with mortification as I weave between silk-clad bodies, putting as much distance between myself and the Duke as the crowded ballroom permits. Of all the people to catch me eavesdropping—the notorious Duke of Westmoreland himself! I'll be fortunate if he doesn't remember my face long enough to mention it to my father.

The sounds of the orchestra wash over me as I scan the crowd for Victoria. My throat feels tight, as it always does in these gatherings where I am so painfully aware of my own inadequacies. There—Victoria stands near the refreshment table, her emerald gown catching the light from the chandeliers, her perfect posture making her appear even taller than she is. I make my way toward her, carefully stepping around dancing couples and conversing groups, none of whom seem to notice my passage.

"There you are, Eleanor," Victoria says as I approach. "I was beginning to think you had found a carriage home without telling me."

"No," I reply softly, "I only needed some air."

Victoria's gaze drifts over my shoulder, and I know she is already searching for more interesting company. I stand firmly beside her anyway, watching couples whirl past in the intricate patterns of a country dance. The gentleman's eyes slide over me as if I were merely an extension of the wallpaper. Not one approaches to request my hand, not even the most desperate of younger sons or aging widowers. I am accustomed to this invisibility, but it stings nonetheless.

I wonder, not for the first time, what it would be like to be Victoria, or Elizabeth, my other elder sister. To be beautiful, sought after, the center of attention in any gathering. To have one's opinion valued, one's presence desired. Victoria's husband appears at her side, whispering something in her ear that makes her laugh, and I feel a pang of envy so sharp it steals my breath.

"Oh! Is that Lady Anne Blackwood?" Victoria suddenly exclaims, her attention caught by a handsome woman across the room. "We came out the same Season, you know. Such a lovely person."

I follow her gaze to see an elegant woman in deep blue silk, perhaps ten years my senior. She has spotted Victoria as well, and her face lights with recognition. They both begin moving toward one another, Victoria pulling me along in her wake.

"Lady Anne! How wonderful to see you again after so long," Victoria gushes when we meet in the center of the ballroom.

"Lady Devonham! I hardly recognized you—marriage clearly agrees with you," Lady Anne responds warmly.

"Indeed, it does. Three children now, can you believe it?"

"Three? How marvelous. I have my three girls, of course. The eldest, Catherine, is sixteen now and already driving her father to distraction with talk of her own coming out."

I stand quietly beside them, forgotten as usual, as they exchange news of families and mutual acquaintances. I allow my mind to drift, imagining the sonata I had been practicing before we left for the ball. The third movement still gives me trouble in the transitions...

"And who is this?" Lady Anne's voice breaks into my thoughts.

Victoria startles slightly, as if she had indeed forgotten I was there. "Oh! Forgive me. This is my sister, Lady Eleanor Hartwood."

I curtsy, feeling Lady Anne's kind but assessing gaze upon me.

"A pleasure to meet you, Lady Eleanor. Are you enjoying the ball?"

"It is a lovely gathering, my lady," I answer politely, the response I have given a hundred times at a hundred similar events.

Before Lady Anne can respond, a tall figure appears behind her, and my stomach drops. The Duke of Westmoreland, his dark eyes surveying the crowd with barely concealed boredom.

"Ah, Sebastian, there you are," Lady Anne says. "Allow me to introduce Lady Devonham, whom I knew as Lady Victoria Hartwood before her marriage, and her sister, Lady Eleanor Hartwood. Ladies, my brother, the Duke of Westmoreland."

He bows slightly, the gesture perfunctory. "Lady Devonham. Lady Eleanor."

His eyes meet mine for the briefest moment, and I find I cannot read his expression. *Is it disinterest? Disdain?* Whatever it is, I am certain he has already forgotten me.

The orchestra begins the opening notes of a waltz, and to my horror, I see Lady Anne give her brother a not-so-subtle nudge with her elbow. His jaw tightens almost imperceptibly.

"Lady Eleanor," he says, his voice deep and controlled, "would you honor me with this dance?"

The question hangs in the air between us like a suspended note. I cannot possibly have heard correctly. Yet Victoria is staring at me with wide eyes, and Lady Anne looks expectant. My mouth has gone dry as parchment.

"I... yes, Your Grace. Thank you."

He offers his arm, and I place my gloved hand upon it, feeling as if I have somehow stepped into another woman's life. As we move toward the dance floor, I become painfully aware of the turning heads, the whispers behind fans. The Duke of Westmoreland, dancing with plain Lady Eleanor Hartwood? The room seems to ripple with shock.

His hand settles at my waist, proper yet commanding, and we join the waltz. I fix my eyes on his cravat, unable to meet his gaze, feeling the weight of every curious stare in the ballroom. My cheeks burn with self-consciousness. This is precisely the sort of attention I have spent my life avoiding, and now it surrounds me like floodwaters.

I grasp the Duke's hand as we move in the prescribed patterns of the waltz, acutely conscious of his every movement, his every breath. My hand feels small and fragile in his, and I focus desperately on counting the steps in my head rather than meeting his eyes. One-two-three, one-two-three. I have danced this pattern a thousand times in empty ballrooms and during endless lessons, yet never has it felt so treacherous.

The whispers that follow us across the floor cut more sharply than any knife. They make no effort to hide their astonishment—or worse, their amusement.

"Is that Lady Eleanor Hartwood with the Duke?"

"Surely not—oh! It is indeed. How extraordinary."

"What could have possessed him to select her, of all people?"

"Perhaps he lost a wager."

That last comment, delivered with a tinkling laugh that carries even over the orchestra, makes me falter slightly. The Duke's hand tightens almost imperceptibly at my waist, steadying me before I can miss a step.

"You dance well, Lady Eleanor," he remarks, his tone neutral. It is the first thing he has said to me since we took to the floor.

"Thank you, Your Grace," I manage to reply, my voice barely audible. "You are most kind."

His expression suggests my assessment of his kindness is questionable, but he says nothing more as we continue to circle the floor.

The music reaches a crescendo, and suddenly partners are exchanged in the intricate pattern of the dance. I find myself momentarily paired with an elderly gentleman who smiles absently at me, clearly untroubled by my plainness. For these few blessed moments, I am free from the Duke's overwhelming presence.

And now, with some distance between us, I can properly observe him once more as he dances with a striking blonde whose face shines with delight at her good fortune. The Duke of Westmoreland is, I must admit, devastatingly handsome in a way that makes my chest ache with something like longing —not for him specifically, but for the impossibility of ever being noticed by a man of such caliber. His movements are fluid and confident, his posture impeccable without appearing stiff. Even the way he holds his head speaks of generations of nobility and the absolute certainty of his place in the world.

Next to him, I am nothing. Less than nothing—I am a curiosity, an oddity that has somehow wandered onto the dance floor by mistake. The thought settles in my stomach like a stone.

The pattern of the dance brings us back together, and I notice something shift in his expression as he takes my hand again. *Is it impatience? Regret at having asked me to dance?* Whatever it is, that fleeting look is enough to shatter what little composure I have maintained.

"Your Grace," I say quietly as we move through the next turn, "I fear I—I am not feeling well. I must beg your pardon."

His eyebrows lift slightly, but before he can respond, I have already slipped my hand from his and am moving away through the crowd, ignoring the startled expressions of the couples around us. I feel his eyes on my back, burning like twin brands, but I do not look back. I cannot.

The crowd parts before me—perhaps the only time in my life they have noticed me enough to do so—and I weave through silk gowns and black coats, desperate to escape the stifling heat of the ballroom, the weight of all those stares. Whispers follow me like trailing ivy.

"Did she just leave the Duke standing there?"

"Most improper..."

"Perhaps she truly is ill?"

"Or perhaps she finally realized how absurd they looked together."

THE VERANDA

I make my way back to the veranda where our paths first crossed, grateful for the cool night air that soothes my burning cheeks. The moon hangs low and full over Lady Harsgrove's gardens, casting cool silver light over the manicured hedges and slumbering roses. I grip the stone balustrade, drawing deep breaths into my constricted lungs.

What have I done? To walk away from a Duke mid-dance—it is beyond improper. It is unheard of. Father will be furious. Victoria will be mortified. And yet, the thought of continuing that dance, of enduring those stares and whispers for even another minute...

I close my eyes, focusing on the distant sound of crickets and the gentle rustle of leaves in the night breeze. Here, at least, there are no judgmental eyes, no whispered insults. Here I can simply be—

"Lady Eleanor."

My eyes fly open at the sound of that deep voice. The Duke stands not three feet away, his tall figure silhouetted against the light from the ballroom. *How did he approach so silently? And why has he followed me?*

"Your Grace," I whisper, instinctively backing up a step. "I—I beg your pardon for my abrupt departure."

He moves closer, into the moonlight, and I can now see his expression. His dark eyes gleam with something that might be anger, might be curiosity.

"Are you unwell?" he asks, his tone clipped. "Or is there

another explanation for why you left me standing alone on the dance floor like a fool?"

I swallow hard, unable to meet his gaze. "I truly am sorry, Your Grace."

"That is not an answer to my question." His voice is cold now, imperial. "I find myself in the unusual position of being publicly abandoned during a dance. I believe I am owed an explanation."

"I—" Words fail me as I glance up at his face, so handsome even in obvious irritation. "The whispers," I finally manage. "I could not bear them."

"Whispers?" One eyebrow arches imperiously. "I was not aware that you were so delicate as to be undone by mere gossip."

His condescension stings, and something within me—some long-dormant spark of pride—flares unexpectedly.

"Not about me, Your Grace. I am quite accustomed to being the object of ridicule. It was the speculation about why someone like you would dance with someone like me that I found unbearable."

"Someone like me?" he repeats, his tone dangerously soft.

"A Duke. A celebrated catch. A man who could have his pick of any woman in that ballroom." I gesture toward the lights and music behind us. "What else could it be but a cruel joke or a lost wager that would prompt you to single out the plainest, most forgettable woman present?"

For a moment, he seems genuinely taken aback by my candor. Then his features harden once more.

"How remarkably self-pitying," he says icily. "And how insulting to me, to assume I acted from such petty motives. Is your opinion of yourself truly so low that you cannot imagine any other reason?"

His question hangs between us, unanswerable. The truth is, I cannot imagine any other reason. Not a single one.

CHAPTER SIX
TEMPEST
THE DUKE OF WESTMORELAND

I wake with a pounding headache, the unfortunate consequence of one too many brandies in the early hours of the morning. The sunshine streaming through my windows feels like a personal affront. My valet, Thompson, has already laid out my morning attire and stands with irritating efficiency at the ready.

"Good morning, Your Grace," he says, his voice mercifully quiet.

I merely grunt in response, allowing him to assist me into my clothing. The events of last evening's ball swirl uncomfortably in my mind—the endless parade of eligible young ladies, their mothers' calculating gazes, and... that quiet, plain girl with the remarkable eyes. What was her name? Eleanor. Lady Eleanor Hartwood, sister to the Countess of Devonham.

"Will you be joining the family for breakfast, sir?" Thompson inquires.

"I suppose I must," I mutter, silently wishing for the solitude of my chambers and a pot of strong coffee.

The breakfast room is indeed a vision of morning chaos when I enter. My sister Anne presides at the head of the table, attempting to maintain some semblance of order while her husband Henry teases their youngest daughter. Their three girls—Catherine, Margaret, and Sophie—chatter simultaneously about entirely different subjects. The noise is nearly unbearable.

"Good morning, Sebastian," Anne calls cheerfully when she spots me. "We were beginning to wonder if you'd join us at all."

Henry glances up with an all-too-knowing smile. "Rough night, old chap?"

I slide into my seat with as much dignity as possible. "Simmons, coffee. Strong. And perhaps something for this blasted headache."

Anne gives me a disapproving glance but says nothing of my language in front of my nieces. Sophie, all of twelve years, giggles behind her napkin. I manage a half-smile for her benefit.

"Catherine, please do not slouch," Anne admonishes her eldest, who promptly straightens her spine. "And Margaret, you know perfectly well that your dancing master expects you to practice for at least an hour today."

"But Mama—"

"No arguments."

I watch my sister in begrudging admiration. She rules this household with a firm but gentle hand, maintaining order among her boisterous family with seemingly effortless grace. Ten years my senior, she stepped into the role of mother after our parents' deaths, guiding me through the responsibilities thrust upon me at too young an age. I sometimes forget how much I owe her.

"Sebastian," she says after a moment, her tone shifting to one I know all too well. "I wonder if I might have a word with you after breakfast? In the library, perhaps?"

I barely suppress a groan. "Another lecture, Anne?"

"Not a lecture," she responds with practiced patience. "A conversation."

Henry catches my eye and gives an almost imperceptible shrug that clearly says: Best to surrender now, old boy.

Half an hour later, I find myself ensconced in the blessed quiet of the library. The coffee has begun to do its work, though my head still throbs in protest at the previous night's excesses. I stand before the window, gazing out at the grounds of Waltham Manor, when Anne enters and closes the door firmly behind her.

"You appeared to be quite... merry when you returned last night," she begins.

"If by 'merry' you mean thoroughly fed up with being paraded before every unmarried female in Yorkshire, then yes, I was exceedingly merry."

Anne sighs and seats herself in one of the leather chairs. "I may have a solution to your dilemma."

"I wasn't aware I had a dilemma beyond an aching head," I reply, turning to face her.

"Sebastian, please be serious for a moment. You know what will happen if you do not secure the succession. Our blasted cousin, Edmund—"

"Do not speak that man's name in my presence." The mere mention of our distant cousin—a dissolute gambler with a penchant for mistreating horses and servants alike—is enough to darken my mood further.

"Then you understand the urgency of your situation. You need a wife."

"So you and half of London society continue to remind me."

Anne ignores my sarcasm. "I had a most enlightening conversation with Victoria, Countess of Devonham, last night."

"The beauty whose Season coincided with yours?" I recall vaguely. "What has she to do with anything?"

"She has a sister. Lady Eleanor Hartwood."

I freeze, memories of the previous night suddenly sharpening. "I danced with her last night."

"I know. I was the one who encouraged you to ask her."

"She's..." I search for a diplomatic description, "...ill-favored."

Anne raises a single eyebrow. "Is she? I found her quite intelligent in our brief exchange."

"Intelligent, perhaps, but she possesses no confidence whatsoever. I've never met a woman who thinks so little of herself." The memory of Lady Eleanor's downcast eyes and hesitant speech returns to me. "She flinched when I merely addressed her directly."

"And that disqualifies her as a potential duchess?" Anne challenges.

I pace before the fireplace. "I cannot see myself married to someone so... so..."

"So unlikely to break your heart?" Anne finishes quietly.

"That is unfair."

"Is it? Sebastian, you do not need to love her. You do not even need to like her, though I suspect you might if you gave yourself the chance. You simply need to *marry* her."

I stare at my sister in disbelief. "You're suggesting I enter a loveless marriage of convenience?"

"I'm suggesting a business arrangement—plain and simple." Anne rises and approaches me. "No heartache like with Seraphina. Just the satisfaction of knowing that Waltham Manor and the dukedom will not fall into the hands of our greedy, gambling cousin."

"And what of Lady Eleanor in all this? Am I to believe she would happily agree to such an arrangement?"

"She's approaching her sixth Season without a single serious suitor. Her family name is impeccable, but her prospects are limited. The title of duchess would be far more than she could hope for otherwise. Her dowry is quite substantial."

I shake my head, unsettled by the cold calculation in Anne's voice—so unlike her usual warmth. "You make it sound so mercenary."

"Marriage among our class often is," she replies simply. "Henry and I were fortunate to find affection in our arrangement. But many do not. And you, brother, after what happened with Seraphina... perhaps it's safer this way."

Her words strike an uncomfortable chord within me. Safer. Less painful. A transaction rather than a vulnerability.

"I'll consider it," I say finally, if only to end this conversation and nurse my aching head in peace.

"Please," Anne asks, while she watches me abruptly stand up. "Where are you off to?"

I wince as the sudden movement sends a fresh wave of pain through my temples. The brandy from last night is exacting its revenge with remarkable efficiency.

"Fresh air," I mutter, straightening my waistcoat with deliberate movements. "This conversation has grown tiresome, and I find myself in need of solitude to contemplate my apparently mercenary future."

The bitterness in my voice surprises even me. Anne means well—she always does—but her clinical dissection of my impending marriage leaves a sour taste that even the lingering effects of last night's indulgence cannot mask.

I leave the library, resisting the urge to slam the door behind me like one of my petulant nieces. Anne's words follow me down the corridor, persistent as my headache. A loveless marriage of convenience. A business arrangement. My life reduced to a transaction to secure the succession.

Thompson appears as if summoned by my darkening mood. "Your riding clothes, Your Grace?"

"Immediately," I reply, grateful for his efficiency. Within minutes, I've exchanged my morning attire for riding breeches and boots. The prospect of escaping these stifling walls, even temporarily, lightens my spirits marginally.

The stable yard bustles with activity when I arrive. Grooms scurry about, attending to their duties with practiced precision. My head groom, Morris, straightens when he spots me.

"Good morning, Your Grace. Will you be taking *Tempest* out today?"

"Indeed." I cannot help the small smile that touches my lips at the mention of my newest acquisition.

Tempest—a magnificent black Arabian I won in a card game just last month from Lord Pembroke, who had been fool enough to wager such a prize. The horse had a reputation for being unmanageable, but I've always had a way with difficult creatures. Within weeks, we've developed an understanding of sorts.

Morris nods knowingly. "He's been restless this morning. A good run would serve him well."

The stallion is brought out, seventeen hands of gleaming muscle and barely contained energy. His dark eyes meet mine with that peculiar intelligence I've come to appreciate. Unlike humans, horses harbor no secret motivations, no hidden agendas. They are creatures of instinct and honesty.

"Good morning, you magnificent beast," I murmur, running a hand along his sleek neck. *Tempest* tosses his head, impatient to be off.

I mount with practiced ease, settling into the saddle as *Tempest* dances beneath me, eager for open ground. With a touch of my heels, we're off, trotting through the stable yard and onto the path that leads to the meadows beyond.

Once we clear the formal gardens, I give him his head. *Tempest* responds instantly, surging forward with explosive power. The countryside flies past in a blur of green and gold, the summer morning alive around us. The wind tears at my hair and clothing, and I find myself laughing aloud at the pure, uncomplicated joy of it. This—this freedom, this mastery, this partnership with a creature of such raw power—this is something I understand.

We thunder across the lower meadows, jumping a stone wall with effortless grace, then begin the climb toward the eastern ridge. *Tempest's* breathing grows heavier but his stride remains strong. I ease him to a walk as we approach the summit, allowing him to recover while we ascend the final stretch.

At the top of the hill, I dismount, giving *Tempest* the freedom to graze while I stand at the edge, gazing out over my lands. From this vantage point, Waltham Manor appears as a toy in the distance, its sandstone walls glowing warmly in the morning light. Beyond lie the villages, farms, and woodlands that comprise the duchy—my responsibility, my burden, my inheritance.

"And apparently reason enough to marry a woman I barely know," I mutter to *Tempest*, who flicks an ear in my direction but continues grazing.

I sink down onto a large, flat stone, my thoughts turning inevitably to Seraphina. Beautiful, vibrant, faithless Seraphina. *Why did she reject me? What did the Marquess of Landry offer that I could not?* I had wealth, title, lands—everything a woman of ambition could desire. I even believed, fool that I was, that we shared genuine affection.

Yet she abandoned me without hesitation, leaving me standing like a pathetic figure of ridicule before all of society. The humiliation burns even now, two years later.

If she had appeared at our wedding, as planned, as promised... I would be a married man now. Perhaps already a father. *Would I be happy?* I had certainly believed so at the time.

Do I still love her?

The question settles uncomfortably in my chest. I pluck a stem of grass, twisting it between my fingers as I force myself to consider it honestly.

No. Whatever I felt for Seraphina has calcified into something harder, colder. Resentment, perhaps. Wounded pride, certainly. But not love.

Yet I miss... *something*. The anticipation of seeing her each day. The warmth of her hand in mine during our walks. The scent of her perfume. The sound of her laughter—though now I wonder if that laughter had often been at my expense.

What is this emptiness, then? This hollow space that makes Anne's suggestion of a practical marriage seem so bleak, yet simultaneously so fitting?

Tempest wanders closer, nudging my shoulder with his velvety nose. I stroke his forelock absently.

"What is it I truly want, old boy?" I ask aloud. "Companionship? The comfort of a warm body beside me at night? An heir to prevent that wretched cousin from inheriting?"

All of those things, yes. But something more eludes me—something I cannot name or perhaps dare not acknowledge.

I stand, brushing grass from my breeches. The sun has climbed higher, and already the day grows warmer. *Tempest* watches me expectantly, ready for our return journey.

"Come," I tell him, gathering the reins. "We cannot hide up here forever, much as we might wish to."

As I mount again, I resolve to consider Anne's suggestion more seriously. Lady Eleanor Hartwood. Plain, shy, unremarkable—and utterly unlikely to inspire the kind of desperate, foolish attachment I once felt for Seraphina.

Perhaps that is precisely what I need.

CHAPTER SEVEN
THE SUN ON HER FACE
LADY ELEANOR HARTWOOD

I stretch my arms toward the warm spring sun, tilting my face to catch its gentle rays. The warmth seeps into my skin like honey, dissolving the lingering chill that had settled in my bones during the night. How different this morning feels from the cold darkness of my bedchamber, where I had lain awake for hours, my thoughts as restless as the wind that rattled against the windowpanes. Now, as the sunlight bathes my features, I feel something inside me soften and unfurl, like a tightly closed blossom finally coaxed open. The coldness—both of the night and of my apprehensions—melts away, if only for this brief, golden moment. The expansive garden of Ravensbrook Hall spreads before me in verdant splendor, dotted with the colorful figures of my nieces and nephews as they dart between flower beds and shrubbery.

"Aunt Eleanor! Watch this!" Richard, Victoria's seven-year-old son, performs a rather wobbly cartwheel that ends with him sprawled inelegantly on the lawn.

"Most impressive," I call back, unable to restrain my smile as he scrambles back to his feet with the resilience only children possess.

My mind wanders treacherously back to last night's ball at Lady Harsgrove's. I can still feel the weight of numerous stares as the Duke of Westmoreland led me onto the dance floor. The pressure of his gloved hand against mine, the perfect distance he maintained between us as we moved through the first figures of the dance.

What possessed me to flee? One moment we were executing the steps with reasonable competence—the next, panic seized my heart. His dark eyes had fixed upon mine with such intensity that I felt stripped bare, as though he could see every inadequacy that marked me as unworthy of his notice.

So I ran. Like a frightened rabbit, I bolted from the ballroom without excuse or explanation, abandoning the most eligible bachelor in England mid-dance. The memory makes me cringe. How mortified he must have been. How angry.

"He will never think of me again except as that peculiar Hartwood girl who lacks even basic manners," I murmur to myself, plucking absently at a blade of grass.

Yet I cannot help but recall the breadth of his shoulders beneath perfectly tailored evening clothes, the subtle scent of sandalwood that clung to him, the unexpected gentleness in hands that guided me through the dance with practiced ease.

Such thoughts are pointless torture. I shall never again stand so close to the Duke of Westmoreland. Never again experience the singular thrill of being the focus of his attention, however briefly. The opportunity came once—a cosmic accident, surely—and I squandered it completely.

"Aunt Eleanor!" This time it is my niece Catherine, Victoria's eldest at nine years old. "Will you play tag with us?"

I hesitate. At three-and-twenty, I am rather past the age for such exertions, but Catherine's expectant face weakens my resolve.

"Very well, but I warn you, I am exceedingly slow."

This declaration is met with delighted squeals as the children circle me like tiny predators. Richard darts forward to tap my arm.

"You're it!" he crows triumphantly before racing away.

I make a halfhearted attempt to give chase, my movements awkward and constrained by my morning dress. The children scatter like startled birds, their laughter trailing behind them. I lunge for little Thomas, miscalculate badly, and find myself falling forward with alarming speed.

The ground rises to meet me with unforgiving firmness. I land sprawled most ungracefully upon the lawn, grass stains undoubtedly marking the pale blue muslin of my gown. The children's laughter redoubles at my predicament

"Lady Eleanor." A footman appears at the edge of the lawn, his expression carefully neutral despite the spectacle I present. "There is a caller for you in the blue drawing room."

"A caller?" I repeat foolishly, still prostrate upon the grass. "For me?"

Before the footman can respond, Victoria's voice cuts across the garden like a well-honed blade.

"Eleanor! Good heavens, what are you doing? Get up this instant!"

I scramble to my feet, brushing ineffectually at the grass and dirt clinging to my gown. Victoria strides toward me, every inch the countess in her perfectly arranged morning costume of lavender silk.

"You have grass in your hair," she hisses, plucking frantically at my disheveled coiffure. "And your gown is ruined. Whatever possessed you to cavort about like a child?"

"I was merely—"

"Never mind that now. You have a caller, Eleanor. A caller! And you look like you've been dragged backward through the shrubbery."

"Who would possibly call upon me?" I ask, genuinely puzzled. In five Seasons, I have received precisely three callers—all gentlemen of advanced age and modest fortune whose interest quickly transferred to more appealing prospects.

Victoria's lips curve into a smile that can only be described as triumphant.

"The Duke of Westmoreland."

The world tilts alarmingly beneath my feet. "That cannot be—"

"I assure you, I have not suddenly gone blind or soft in the head." Victoria seizes my arm, propelling me toward the house with surprising strength. "He is waiting in the blue drawing room, and you look absolutely disreputable. We must get you upstairs immediately."

"But why would he call on me? After last night—"

"After last night, I imagined he might never speak to any of us again," Victoria admits, tugging me up the garden steps. "Your behavior was incomprehensible, Eleanor. But evidently the Duke found something of interest, despite your best efforts to humiliate yourself. Now, for the love of all that is holy, do not keep him waiting while we debate his motives!"

My heart pounds with painful intensity. The Duke of Westmoreland, here? To see me? It defies all logic and expectation. Perhaps he has come to demand an explanation for my rudeness. Perhaps he means to upbraid me publicly for my appalling manners.

Or perhaps—but no, I must not indulge in fantasy. Whatever his purpose, I must face him—grass stains, disheveled hair, and all.

I have exactly five minutes to transform from garden ragamuffin to presentable lady. The maid Victoria summons works with frantic efficiency, stripping my soiled gown and replacing it with a fresh muslin day dress in palest yellow. My hair proves more challenging—loose tendrils escape her attempts at tidying, and I can see in the looking glass that several blades of grass remain stubbornly entangled despite her ministrations.

"No more time, my lady," she whispers apologetically, securing one last hairpin.

Victoria appears in the doorway, her expression vacillating between hope and exasperation. "It will have to do. He's been waiting nearly ten minutes already."

"Perhaps I should send word that I am indisposed—"

"You will do no such thing." She seizes my elbow, propelling me toward the stairs. "This may be your only opportunity to make amends for last night's debacle."

"I do not understand why he would call upon me—"

"Men of his standing rarely require logical explanations for their actions, Eleanor. Now, chin up. Try to look at least marginally pleased to see him."

Before I can formulate another protest, Victoria practically pushes me through the drawing room door, closing it firmly behind me.

The Duke of Westmoreland stands by the window, his tall figure silhouetted against the bright garden beyond. He turns at my entrance, and I watch his expression transform from polite expectancy to undisguised surprise.

His dark eyes widen as they track from my hastily arranged hair—where I know at least one grass blade remains visible—down to my fresh but hastily donned gown. I feel heat bloom across my cheeks under his scrutiny, an intense inspection that seems to catalog every imperfection, every sign of my recent garden adventure.

I stand frozen, painfully aware of my inadequacies. Next to his immaculate appearance—the perfectly tailored morning coat of finest blue superfine, the pristine cravat arranged in an intricate knot—I must appear positively feral.

The silence stretches between us, growing more uncomfortable with each passing second. *Why has he come?* After my shameful flight from the ballroom last evening, I expected never to encounter him again, certainly not in my own home, with grass in my hair and my composure in tatters.

"Lady Eleanor." His voice, when he finally speaks, is deeper than I remember, with an undertone I cannot quite interpret. "I trust I find you well this morning?"

"Yes, Your Grace. Thank you." The words emerge sounding strangled and formal.

He moves away from the window, taking two steps toward me before halting at a proper distance. His eyes continue their assessment, lingering on my hair with something that might be amusement hidden in their depths.

"I wished to—" He pauses, seeming suddenly less certain than his commanding presence would suggest. "That is, I wondered if you might care to take a turn about the gardens? The weather is exceptionally fine today."

Of all possible reasons for his call, this request is so unexpected that I find myself momentarily speechless. *A walk? With the Duke of Westmoreland? After I abandoned him on the dance floor without explanation?*

"I—" What can I possibly say? Yes would be presumptuous; no would be insulting. While I struggle to formulate a response that will not further humiliate me, fate intervenes in the form of a small hurricane of children.

The drawing room door bursts open, and my nieces and nephews tumble in like puppies, heedless of propriety or the presence of one of England's most distinguished peers.

"Aunt Eleanor!" Richard seizes my hand, tugging insistently. "You promised to finish our game! We've been waiting forever!"

Catherine attaches herself to my other arm. "Thomas says you weren't really 'it' when you fell, but you were! Tell him you were!"

"Children!" I attempt to extricate myself from their grasp, mortified beyond words. "We have a visitor. His Grace, the Duke of—"

"Are you coming to play with us too, sir?" Little Thomas peers up at the Duke with innocent curiosity.

For a moment—just a fleeting moment—something softens in the Duke's expression as he gazes down at my nephew. Then, like a candle snuffed by a sudden draft, it vanishes, replaced by the cool, distant demeanor I observed at Lady Harsgrove's ball.

"I see you have prior engagements, Lady Eleanor." He offers a slight bow, already retreating toward the door. "I shall not impose upon your time any further."

"Your Grace.' But what can I say? The children continue to pull at my arms, chattering about the abandoned game in the garden.

"Good day." With those curt words, he strides from the room, each step purposeful and swift. I stand paralyzed, unable to follow, trapped by both the children's grip and the knowledge that nothing I could say would repair whatever fragile opportunity had presented itself and shattered in the space of minutes.

The front door closes with a distant thud. Through the drawing room window, I watch him walking down the drive, his back straight, his steps measured. He does not look back.

Something tightens in my chest—a peculiar ache unlike anything I have experienced before. It feels remarkably like loss, which makes no sense at all. *How can one lose something one never possessed?*

"Aunt Eleanor?" Catherine's voice penetrates my reverie. "Why do you look so sad?"

I turn from the window, forcing my lips into a smile that feels brittle enough to crack my face.

"I am not sad, darling." The lie tastes bitter on my tongue. "Let us return to our game."

But as I allow the children to lead me back to the garden, I cannot shake the hollow feeling that settles in my stomach. For a brief, inexplicable moment, something possible had stood before me—something I had not even known to wish for—and now it has walked away, as unreachable as the stars that will appear in tonight's sky.

My fingers curl reflexively around Catherine's small hand as she tugs me toward the far side of the lawn where the others await.

"Come, Aunt Eleanor! You promised another game!"

I follow her without truly seeing the path before me, my mind still trapped in those moments in the drawing room, replaying every second, every expression that crossed the Duke's face. Had I imagined that brief softening when he looked at Thomas? Perhaps it was merely a trick of the light through the windows. Perhaps I saw what I wished to see—a glimpse of something warmer beneath his polished exterior.

"You must catch us now!" Richard shouts, dancing away from me with childish glee.

I make a halfhearted lunge in his direction, my thoughts elsewhere entirely. *Why did he come?* The question circles my mind like a relentless falcon. The Duke of Westmoreland has no reason to seek my company. At Lady Harsgrove's ball last evening, he must have been introduced to dozens of eligible young women—each one prettier, more accomplished, more worthy of his attention than I.

Yet he came here. To Ravensbrook Hall. To call upon *me*.

"Aunt Eleanor, you're not even trying!" Thomas complains as I stand motionless in the middle of the lawn.

"Forgive me, children." I shake my head, trying to dislodge these useless wonderings. "I am a bit distracted today."

I make a more convincing effort at the game, chasing the children around a flowering shrub, but my heart remains absent from the activity. Perhaps, I think as I feign pursuit, the Duke's call was merely a courtesy. An obligation he felt toward an awkward dance partner who fled from his presence. The thought settles heavy in my stomach. Yes, that seems most likely. A gentleman of his standing would feel compelled to ensure no lasting harm had been done.

Catherine shrieks with delight as I capture her around the waist, lifting her briefly before setting her down again. "Now you're it, Catherine! Count to twenty while we hide!"

As the children scatter, I move to the shade of an ancient oak tree, grateful for a moment's respite. My fingers brush against the rough bark, seeking its solid reassurance. The Duke's expression when he first turned from the window haunts me —that look of surprise giving way to something else. Something I cannot name because I dare not.

You are being ridiculous, Eleanor. I scold myself silently. *A man like the Duke of Westmoreland could never look at you with genuine interest. You are plain, unremarkable, lacking in every quality that might capture and hold his attention.*

This harsh assessment brings no pain—it is merely truth, reinforced by years of evidence. Even my father sees it clearly. "Too plain for a good match," he had declared just days ago, the words delivered with the casual cruelty of undisputed fact.

Catherine finishes her counting and begins searching for her siblings. I remain beneath the oak, temporarily forgotten in the excitement of the hunt. Through the dappled shade, I watch clouds drift across the spring sky, their edges gilded by sunlight. It occurs to me that I should feel something more than this dull resignation. I should feel humiliated by the Duke's visit—by the state in which he found me, by the children's interruption—but oddly, I do not.

Instead, I feel a curious emptiness, as though something I never knew I wanted has slipped through my fingers before I could recognize its value.

A commotion near the house draws my attention. Victoria has emerged onto the veranda, but rather than her usual measured progress, she is moving with surprising speed, her skirts gathered in her hands as she hurries down the garden steps. Her composure—usually as immaculate as her appearance—seems to have abandoned her entirely. She stumbles slightly on the sloping lawn, catching herself before continuing her headlong rush toward me.

"Eleanor!" Her voice carries across the garden, startling a pair of doves from a nearby bush. "Eleanor!"

I step away from the tree, alarm rising within me. *Has something happened? Is someone ill?*

Victoria's face is flushed, her carefully arranged coiffure beginning to loosen with each rapid step. The children pause in their game, watching with wide eyes as their usually dignified mother races across the lawn like a girl of sixteen.

"Eleanor!" She reaches me, breathing heavily, her hands grasping my arms with unexpected force. "You will *never*—I can scarcely believe—oh, Eleanor!"

"Victoria, what is it?" I steady her, concern mounting at her incoherence. "Has something happened?"

She nods frantically, struggling to catch her breath. "Yes! Something has happened! Something extraordinary!"

"Are you ill? Is it Father?"

"No, no! Nothing like that!" She laughs, a sound of pure astonishment. "It's the Duke!"

My heart performs a curious little stumble. "The Duke is ill?"

"No-no, silly girl," Victoria's eyes are wide, her expression wavering between disbelief and delight. "He's with Father now, in the library. Eleanor, he asked to speak with him privately the moment you left the drawing room!"

"I do not understand." But a strange fluttering begins in my stomach, a sensation so unfamiliar I can hardly identify it.

"Eleanor!" Victoria gives my arms a little shake, as though trying to rouse me from slumber. "The Duke of Westmoreland has asked Father for your hand in marriage!"

The world seems to tilt beneath me. "That cannot be—"

"It is! I heard it with my own ears! I was passing the library door—" Here she has the grace to look slightly abashed for eavesdropping. "He spoke quite plainly. He wishes to marry you, Eleanor. You! He has asked Father's permission to court you with the explicit intention of making you his duchess!"

I stare at her, unable to form words. This cannot be real. Such things do not happen to unremarkable girls like me. Dukes do not propose to the plain, forgettable daughters of earls. They marry beauty, wealth, connections—not quiet shadows who flee from ballrooms in panic.

"There must be some mistake," I finally manage to whisper.

Victoria's smile widens until it threatens to split her face. "No mistake, sister. By summer's end, you shall be the Duchess of Westmoreland."

CHAPTER EIGHT
THREE STONE DOLPHINS
THE DUKE OF WESTMORELAND

I wave a hand dismissively at my driver, ordering the carriage to halt. We've reached the outskirts of my estate, but the notion of being conveyed directly to my front door suddenly feels insufferable.

"I'll walk from here," I announce, stepping down without waiting for assistance. "Continue on. I shall arrive shortly."

My driver's perplexed expression is visible even in the fading twilight. "As you wish, Your Grace."

The wheels crunch against the gravel as the carriage pulls away, and I am left with nothing but the sound of my own footsteps and the disquieting thoughts that have plagued me since departing Ravensbrook Hall.

A mile's walk might clear my head. I loosen my cravat slightly, allowing myself this small freedom now that I'm beyond society's scrutinizing gaze. The evening air carries the scent of earth and greenery—a welcome respite after hours spent in Lord Hartwood's oppressively formal drawing room.

Good God, what have I done?

I replay my conversation with Lord Hartwood, each remembered word making my stomach churn anew.

"Lady Eleanor?" Lord Hartwood had repeated, his eyebrows nearly disappearing into his hairline. "You wish to marry my Eleanor?"

The emphasis he placed on "my" had been almost imperceptible. The emphasis on "Eleanor," however, rang with unmistakable incredulity.

"Indeed, my lord." I had maintained my composure, though my jaw clenched slightly at his tone. "I find her... refreshing."

It wasn't entirely a lie. What I found refreshing was her complete lack of artifice. No calculated glances. No strategic placement of a hand upon my arm. No rehearsed laughter at my lackluster attempts at humor.

"Refreshing?" Lord Hartwood had stared at me as if I'd suggested we hold the wedding ceremony underwater. "Are you quite certain you haven't confused Eleanor with Elizabeth? Elizabeth is recently widowed, of course, but she—"

"I am perfectly aware of which daughter I am requesting permission to marry." My voice had emerged colder than I intended.

Lord Hartwood leaned forward, lowering his voice conspiratorially. "Forgive my impertinence, Your Grace, but I must ask... are you well? Perhaps suffering from some ailment of the mind? A fever, perhaps?"

I had to bite the inside of my cheek to prevent myself from responding in a manner unbefitting my station. It was becoming abundantly clear where Lady Eleanor's evident lack of self-worth originated.

"I assure you, my faculties are entirely intact."

"Well," Lord Hartwood had said, clearing his throat, "I cannot imagine why you would—but who am I to question the Duke of Westmoreland? Eleanor has no other prospects, certainly. Not at her age, and with her... limitations. If you're determined, then of course you have my blessing."

Limitations. The word echoes in my mind now as I stride across the rolling fields of my estate. *What precisely did he mean? That she lacks the classical beauty of her sisters? That she possesses a quieter disposition? That she does not simper and flirt and manipulate as Seraphina had done?*

My boot comes down hard on a stone, and I curse under my breath. There she is again, worming her way into my thoughts. Seraphina. No matter how I try to exorcise her, she remains, a persistent ghost haunting the corners of my mind.

But today, the memory that surfaces isn't of Seraphina's betrayal. It's of Lady Eleanor, standing awkwardly in her father's drawing room, looking as though she'd been dragged through a hedge backward.

She had appeared suddenly, summoned by a servant. I'd turned to find her in the doorway, brown hair escaping its pins in several directions, her day dress rumpled, and—most remarkably—what appeared to be blades of grass tangled in her dark locks.

"Your Grace," she'd said, dropping into a hasty curtsy, her eyes widening with evident mortification as she recognized me. "I... forgive my appearance. I was not expecting visitors."

I'd bitten back a laugh—not of mockery, but of genuine amusement. She looked like some woodland creature, disheveled and authentic in a way that society women never allowed themselves to be seen. For a moment, I glimpsed something beyond the reticent young woman I'd danced with—something vital and unguarded.

Before I could respond, the drawing room doors had burst open again, and three small children had tumbled in, clearly in pursuit of their aunt.

"Aunt Eleanor! You promised us a story!" The smallest one, a girl of perhaps four years, had tugged insistently at Lady Eleanor's skirts.

"Children!" Lord Hartwood's voice had cracked like a whip. "Remove yourselves at once! Can you not see that your aunt is disgracing herself quite thoroughly without your assistance?"

The children had scattered, and Lady Eleanor's face had flushed a deep crimson. Yet the momentary glimpse I'd caught of her with those children—her face alight with genuine warmth—had revealed more of her character than our entire dance at Lady Harsgrove's ball.

What is wrong with this family? How have they failed to see what stands before them?

I slow my pace as Waltham Manor comes into view, its stone facade glowing amber in the setting sun. The grandeur of my ancestral home usually fills me with pride, but tonight it looks merely imposing—cold, even.

What is wrong with me? Why did I propose this arrangement? A marriage of convenience need not be with someone so... overlooked. I could have chosen any number of suitable candidates. Young ladies with impeccable lineage, substantial dowries, and the kind of beauty that turns heads in ballrooms across London.

Yet none of them would have been safe. All would eventually reveal themselves to be like Seraphina—calculating, false, interested only in my title and fortune.

Lady Eleanor Hartwood, with her downcast eyes and grass in her hair, would expect nothing from me beyond the protection of my name. She would not pretend affection only to abandon me for a better prospect. She would be grateful.

I stop walking, suddenly disgusted with myself. *Is that truly my reasoning?* That I seek someone so beaten down by her family's disregard that she would be grateful for a loveless marriage to a cynical Duke?

Perhaps Lord Hartwood was right to question my sanity after all.

I trudge the final steps across the gravel drive until the fountain comes into view. My ancestors commissioned the ostentatious thing—Poseidon with his trident, riding triumphant above ocean waves, water streaming from the mouths of three stone dolphins. I've always found it vulgar, yet tonight I'm drawn to its constant murmur, so unlike the cacophony of my thoughts.

I lower myself onto the stone rim, uncaring that my expensive tailcoat might be ruined. The water beckons, and I dip my hand in, watching ripples disturb the smooth surface. The cool sensation against my skin provides momentary relief from the suffocating weight of what I've done.

I've proposed marriage to Lady Eleanor Hartwood.

My eyes drift closed as water drips from my fingertips. What would life have been like if Seraphina had kept her word? I would be married by now, perhaps even with a child on the way. Our London townhouse would be the epicenter of society, our country estate filled with laughter and music and all those trappings of domestic felicity that poets insist constitute happiness.

And yet.

Even in these imagined scenes, Seraphina's laugh rings false. Her smiles never quite reach her eyes. I envision myself slowly realizing that her affection extends only as far as my fortune. *Would I have discovered this before or after we wed? Before or after a child?* The thought of being trapped in such a marriage sends a chill through me that has nothing to do with the evening air.

I swirl my hand through the water again, watching moonlight dance across the ripples.

And what of Lady Eleanor? What awaits me in *that* future?

A quiet existence, certainly. No grand balls or excessive entertainments. Those hold little appeal for me now, regardless. My estate will run smoothly under her management—this much seems certain. She strikes me as practical, sensible. There will be no excessive spending, no frivolous demands. She will be... suitable.

The word sits uneasily in my mind. *Suitable*. As one might describe a particularly unremarkable horse or an adequate bottle of wine.

Further images form unbidden: Eleanor sitting silently across from me at breakfast, her eyes downcast; Eleanor withdrawing to separate quarters after fulfilling her marital obligations with dutiful submission; Eleanor bearing my children with the same quiet resignation she seems to bring to all aspects of her existence. No spark. No passion. No challenge.

A passive acceptance of whatever scraps of attention I might deign to throw her way.

God, what a bleak picture. And how supremely unfair to her.

She didn't seek this arrangement. I imposed it upon her through her father, who practically pushed her at me like an unwanted parcel. *Will she even have the courage to refuse? Or will she accept my offer with the same weary acquiescence with which she seems to endure her family's casual cruelty?*

I splash the water more forcefully, destroying the calm surface.

"Your Grace?"

My head butler stands a respectful distance away, his face betraying only the slightest curiosity at finding his employer sullying himself at the fountain like a common laborer.

"Lady Anne inquires whether you will be joining her for dinner this evening."

"Yes, Simmons. I'll be along shortly."

He bows and retreats toward the house, his footsteps fading on the gravel path.

I rise to my feet, brushing ineffectually at my damp sleeve. Anne will immediately notice my dishevelment and draw her own conclusions. She'll be delighted to hear that I've secured Lord Hartwood's permission, of course. This arrangement was her idea, after all—her solution to our inheritance predicament.

It is, I remind myself, a sound business decision. The estate will remain in the family line. My insufferable cousin, Mr. Edmund Hanbury—with his gambling debts and his endless schemes—will be denied the satisfaction of inheriting what generations of my family have built. Lady Eleanor will gain the security of a title and wealth. I will gain an undemanding wife who expects nothing more than what I'm willing to provide.

A tidy exchange. A rational choice.

And if some small, obstinate part of me rebels against this cold pragmatism—I shall simply ignore it, as I've learned to ignore so many unwanted feelings these past years.

I pause at the entrance to my ancestral home, glancing back at the fountain where moonlight now dances alone on undisturbed water. So this is to be my life: a title, an estate preserved, a suitable wife, eventual heirs. All the requirements of my position fulfilled with clinical precision.

It should feel like victory. Instead, as I push open the heavy door and step into the echoing entrance hall, I am struck by how closely the future I've chosen resembles the mausoleum-like emptiness of this grand house—impressive from without, yet hollow within.

I pause outside the dining room, my hand poised to push open the heavy oak door. The sounds of merriment filter through—my sister's bell-like laughter, Henry's deeper chuckle, and the girlish giggles of my nieces. Their voices blend together in a melody of family harmony that strikes an unexpected chord within me.

For a moment, I simply listen, unable—or perhaps unwilling—to interrupt their joy with my presence.

"Papa, you cannot possibly mean it!" Catherine's voice rings clearly, her sixteen years lending her tone a newfound authority she tests at every opportunity.

"I assure you, my darling skeptic, the horse truly did wander into the assembly rooms!" Henry's voice carries that particular warmth he reserves exclusively for his daughters.

"In the middle of the cotillion?" Anne asks, her voice suffused with fond exasperation. "Henry, your tales grow more outlandish with each telling."

"The truth requires no embellishment, my love." The affection in Henry's voice is unmistakable, even through solid oak.

A peculiar sensation settles in my chest as I stand there, invisible and apart from their circle of contentment. It isn't quite envy—that would be beneath my dignity—and yet... they share something I have never known. A bond forged through years of genuine affection rather than obligation or advantage.

They have built something real together, something that brings them true happiness.

Will I ever experience such uncomplicated joy? Will my house ever echo with laughter rather than the hollow sound of my solitary footsteps? With Eleanor as my wife, is such a future even possible?

I straighten my shoulders and push the thought away. Such maudlin reflections are unworthy of a Duke.

I push open the door, plastering a mask of ducal indifference over my features.

"Good evening, all." I stride to my customary place at the head of the table. "I trust I haven't delayed dinner overlong."

"Sebastian!" Anne smiles warmly. "We were beginning to wonder if you'd abandoned us for the evening."

"Uncle Sebastian!" My youngest niece, Sophie, bounces slightly in her chair, her twelve-year-old exuberance as yet untamed by the rigid strictures of society. "Did you know Papa once danced with a horse?"

"I suspect your father is exercising his talent for storytelling again." I take my seat as a footman appears at my elbow with a crystal decanter. "Brandy, thank you."

"A particularly fine evening for brandy, is it?" Henry quirks an eyebrow at me, his perceptive gaze noting my slightly disheveled appearance. "Or perhaps a particularly trying afternoon?"

I take a fortifying sip before responding. "Actually, I've had a rather productive day." I allow the statement to hang in the air for a dramatic moment. Why not enjoy this rare opportunity to surprise them all? "I've asked for Lady Eleanor Hartwood's hand in marriage."

The reaction is everything I could have hoped for. Anne's fork clatters against her plate. Henry chokes slightly on his wine. Catherine and Margaret exchange wide-eyed glances, while little Sophie's mouth forms a perfect 'O' of astonishment.

"You've done what?" Anne manages, her composure momentarily shattered.

"I've secured Lord Hartwood's permission to marry his daughter." I cut into my roast beef with deliberate precision, feigning absorption in the task. "You were right, Anne. Lady Eleanor is a perfectly sensible choice. Her family connections are impeccable, she appears capable of managing a household, and she is unlikely to make excessive demands upon my time or attention."

"Good God, Sebastian." Henry's expression hovers somewhere between amusement and horror. "Did you actually present your suit in those terms?"

I frown slightly. "I was considerably more diplomatic in my address to Lord Hartwood, naturally."

"But Eleanor herself..." Anne leans forward, her eyes searching my face. "Did she accept your proposal with joy? Was she pleased?"

I take another sip of brandy, suddenly finding the amber liquid intensely interesting. "I have not yet formally proposed to Lady Eleanor herself."

"Sebastian!" Anne's voice rises sharply. All pretense of dinner forgotten, she stares at me in undisguised dismay. "You asked her father without first securing her affections? Without even speaking to her directly?"

I feel a flush of irritation creeping up my neck. "That is the traditional approach, is it not? I spoke with her father, who was... eventually agreeable to the match."

"Eventually agreeable?" Henry repeats, a troubling twinkle in his eye.

"He may have initially suspected I was suffering from a brain fever," I admit dryly, "but he came around to the idea soon enough."

Anne presses her fingertips against her temples. "So you have arranged a marriage with a young woman who has no idea of your intentions, whose father was skeptical enough to question your sanity, and who has not given her consent to this arrangement?"

When she puts it that way, it does sound rather less than ideal.

"I'm merely following established protocol," I insist, though the words sound hollow even to my own ears. "Her father's blessing is the essential legal requirement."

"Legal requirement!" Anne looks positively indignant now. "Marriage is not merely a legal contract, Sebastian. This is a woman's entire life you're arranging without her knowledge or consent!"

"I fully intend to speak with her—"

"You will call upon her tomorrow," Anne declares, her tone brooking no argument. "You will present yourself properly, speak to her privately, and ask for her hand in marriage like a gentleman. If she accepts—and only if she accepts—will this engagement proceed."

I slouch slightly in my chair, feeling remarkably like a schoolboy being scolded. "I hardly think such dramatics are necessary."

Henry doesn't even attempt to hide his amusement. "On the contrary, I think your sister's suggestion is eminently reasonable. Unless, of course, you fear the lady might refuse you?"

"Don't be absurd," I snap. "Why would she refuse? I'm offering her the protection of my name and title, the security of my fortune, and a position in society far above what she might reasonably expect."

"My," Henry murmurs, "how could any woman resist such a romantic entreaty?"

The girls giggle behind their napkins, and I shoot them a quelling glance that fails entirely to quell.

"Fine," I concede ungraciously. "I shall call upon Lady Eleanor tomorrow and propose properly. Are you satisfied?"

"Nearly." Anne's stern expression softens slightly. "Just promise me you'll approach her with sincerity and kindness, Sebastian. She deserves that much, at least."

I nod curtly, returning my attention to my neglected dinner. The conversation gradually shifts to other topics, but I remain largely silent, brooding over the prospect of tomorrow's obligatory courtship ritual.

How precisely does one propose to a woman one barely knows? What words would convince Lady Eleanor Hartwood that a loveless marriage to me would be preferable to her current existence?

And why does the thought of her potential refusal disturb my composure far more than it reasonably should?

CHAPTER NINE
BUTTERCUP
LADY ELEANOR HARTWOOD

I cannot sleep. Not a wink, not a moment's rest, not even the briefest respite from my circling thoughts. My bedsheets twist around my legs like serpents, evidence of my restlessness. The canopy above my bed, once a comforting shelter, now seems to press down, trapping my tumultuous thoughts within.

Why me?

The question pulses through my mind with each heartbeat. Why would the Duke of Westmoreland—choose me? I am no great beauty like Victoria. I possess no particular wit like Elizabeth. I am simply... Eleanor. Unremarkable Eleanor with grass-stained skirts and unruly hair.

I roll to my side, watching as the first pale fingers of dawn stretch across the horizon. My window faces east, a choice I made years ago when I discovered how the morning light makes the dew-covered gardens shimmer like scattered diamonds. Even exhaustion cannot dull my appreciation for such simple beauty.

Perhaps it is a jest. A cruel game perpetrated by bored members of the ton. Or perhaps he lost a wager. "Marry the plainest girl at Lady Harsgrove's ball." What other explanation could there be?

"You should be honored," Father had said after the Duke departed yesterday, his tone suggesting surprise mingled with disbelief. "I cannot fathom what caught his eye, but you would be a fool to refuse him."

A fool. I have been called worse, though seldom to my face.

The memory of my family's reactions curdles in my stomach. Victoria's wide eyes, her mouth forming a perfect "O" of astonishment. Elizabeth's sudden scrutiny, as though searching for some previously overlooked quality that might explain the Duke's interest. Father's immediate acceptance, as though desperate to secure the match before the Duke could reconsider.

Not one of them asked if I wished to accept.

The door to my bedchamber swings open with a familiar creak, and Wallace bustles in, her sturdy frame silhouetted against the hallway light.

"Up with ye now, my lady! 'Tis a fine mornin' to be alive!" Her Scottish brogue fills the room as she throws open the curtains with enthusiastic abandon. The full force of morning light floods in, and I squint against its sudden brightness.

"I was already awake, Wallace," I murmur, pushing myself into a sitting position.

"Aye, and ye look it too." She clucks her tongue, eyeing the disarray of my bedding. "Did ye sleep at all, then?"

"I found it... difficult."

"Well, ye've cause for excitement, have ye not?" Wallace moves about the room with practiced efficiency, laying out my morning dress and preparing my wash basin. "The whole house is abuzz. A Duke! And not just any Duke, but Westmoreland himself!"

"Yes, quite remarkable." My fingers twist in the sheets. "I still cannot—"

"What's this?" Wallace pauses by my writing desk, lifting a cream-colored envelope with a distinctive wax seal. "It arrived with the early post. One of the footmen brought it up not five minutes ago."

My heart lurches painfully in my chest. "From whom?"

"The Duke's seal, if I'm not mistaken." She crosses to my bed and extends the letter. "Seems your gentleman is an early riser."

"He is not my gentleman," I protest weakly, though I accept the letter with trembling fingers.

"Not yet, perhaps." Wallace's weathered face creases with a knowing smile.

I break the seal with care, unfolding the elegant stationery. The handwriting is bold and decisive, each letter formed with precision.

> Lady Eleanor,
>
> I hope this letter finds you well after yesterday's unexpected discussions. I would be honored if you would join me for a morning ride through Ravensbrook's eastern woods. The weather promises to be fair, and I am told the bluebells are particularly fine this year.
>
> I shall call at ten o'clock, if that is convenient.
>
> Your servant,
> Westmoreland

"Oh!" The exclamation escapes me before I can contain it.

"Good news, then?" Wallace peers at me with undisguised curiosity.

"He wishes me to accompany him riding. Today. At ten o'clock." My voice sounds strange to my ears, higher than usual and tinged with panic.

"Well, that's lovely, isn't it? A chance to become better acquainted before the wedding."

I bolt upright so suddenly that Wallace takes a startled step backward. "Riding, Wallace! On horseback!"

"Aye, that's generally how it's done," she says dryly.

"But I have not been on a horse in years! Not since that dreadful incident with Father's new stallion when I was sixteen." The memory of that humiliation still burns—tumbling from the saddle in front of half the county, my skirts flying up around my waist. "I shall make a complete fool of myself."

"Nonsense. It's not something ye forget."

"It has been seven years!" I scramble from the bed, nearly tripping over the twisted sheets. "Seven years, Wallace! And now the Duke—who probably rides as though he was born in the saddle—wishes me to accompany him. I shall fall. Or the horse shall bolt. Or both!"

"Ye need to breathe, my lady," Wallace says firmly, gripping my shoulders. "In through the nose, out through the mouth."

I obey automatically, my chest rising and falling in measured counts.

"That's better. Now, first things first. We'll need to find your riding habit. I believe it's in the cedar chest, though it may need pressing."

"Perhaps I could suggest a walk instead?" I offer weakly.

"And have him think ye afraid? Is that the impression ye wish to make on your future husband?"

"He is not yet—"

"He will be," Wallace says with such conviction that I find

myself momentarily silenced. "Now, let's see about breakfast. Ye'll need your strength."

* * *

The early morning air carries a crisp promise as I inhale deeply, attempting to steady my nerves. Father's stables have always been a place of comfort for me, despite my unfortunate history with riding. The familiar scents of hay, leather, and horses provide an odd reassurance as I stroke the sleek neck of the gentle mare selected for my ride.

"You'll be kind to me, won't you, *Buttercup*?" I murmur, smoothing my gloved hand along her chestnut coat. "No sudden movements or galloping, if you please. I must appear... competent."

My riding habit, unearthed from the depths of my wardrobe and hastily pressed by Wallace, fits more snugly than I remember. The deep forest green fabric complements my coloring better than I expected, though the cut is perhaps a season or two out of fashion. Wallace assured me I look "perfectly presentable," which from her, is high praise indeed.

"I have never done this before," I confess to *Buttercup*, who regards me with large, liquid eyes. "A courtship, I mean. Though I suppose that's what this is, isn't it? Or perhaps merely a formality before an arrangement is finalized."

The stable is mercifully empty of grooms or stable boys. I had slipped out of the house early, unable to bear Victoria's endless instructions or Elizabeth's fussing over my appearance. The thought of waiting primly in the drawing room, being announced like some prize heifer at market, was more than I could stomach.

"He is a Duke," I remind *Buttercup*, adjusting my hat nervously. "And I am... well, I am, *me*. Surely there must be some mistake."

Buttercup tosses her head and nudges my shoulder with surprising gentleness, as though understanding my anxiety. I laugh despite myself, the tight knot in my chest loosening just a fraction.

"Are you offering encouragement? How very—"

The distinctive sound of hoofbeats silences me mid-sentence. I freeze, then instinctively step behind *Buttercup's* substantial form as a magnificent black stallion appears in the stable entrance, bearing an equally impressive rider.

The Duke of Westmoreland sits astride his mount with an ease I can only envy, his tall frame perfectly balanced and his posture impeccable. The morning sun catches in his dark hair, highlighting unexpected auburn undertones. His riding coat, impeccably tailored of fine blue wool, emphasizes the breadth of his shoulders.

My mouth goes dry. How absurd that I should be hiding like a child caught stealing sweets. Yet I cannot make myself step forward.

The Duke's gaze sweeps the stable and finds me immediately, my hiding place woefully inadequate. Instead of dismounting, he guides his stallion toward me with expert precision, stopping a respectful distance away.

"Lady Eleanor," he says, his voice carrying easily across the space between us. "You surprise me. I had expected to call at the house."

I force myself to step into view, smoothing my hands nervously down my skirts. "Your Grace." I drop into a curtsy, feeling awkward and ungainly. "I... that is... I thought it simpler to meet here."

When I look up, I find him studying me with an intensity that brings heat to my cheeks. From my position below, he appears almost regal, framed by the slanting morning light—like a king surveying his domain.

"You look well," he observes. "That shade of green suits you."

The compliment, however politely delivered, intensifies my blush. "Thank you, Your Grace."

"Are you ready to depart?" he asks, glancing at *Buttercup*. "Do you require assistance mounting?"

My eyes dart around the stable, suddenly aware of our solitude. "The stable boy was here just moments ago," I lie, mortification washing over me. Where have all the servants disappeared to? "I'm certain he'll return shortly."

The Duke's mouth curves slightly as he swings himself down from his saddle with effortless grace. "No matter. I am perfectly capable of assisting you."

Before I can protest, he approaches and stands beside *Buttercup*, lacing his fingers together to create a step for my foot.

BUTTERCUP

"I—" I hesitate, acutely aware of the impropriety. Yet what choice do I have? "Thank you."

I place my boot in his cupped hands, feeling the strength in his grip as he boosts me upward. His other hand steadies me at the waist as I settle into the saddle, his touch sending an unfamiliar tingling sensation through my body. No one has touched me with such casual confidence before—certainly no gentleman. The sensation is shockingly intimate, even through layers of clothing.

I barely have time to arrange my skirts properly before *Buttercup*, apparently tired of waiting, lurches forward without command. A startled cry escapes me as the mare breaks into an immediate trot, then a canter, heading straight for the open stable doors.

"Pull back on the reins!" the Duke shouts behind me, but my hands have frozen in panic. The ground moves alarmingly beneath me as *Buttercup* increases her speed.

I hear the thundering hooves of the Duke's stallion before I see him, and suddenly he appears alongside me, reaching across to grasp *Buttercup*'s reins. With firm, confident hands, he slows both our mounts to a walk.

"Lady Eleanor," he says, his voice tight with concern. "Are you injured?"

"Only my pride," I manage to gasp, my heart hammering against my ribs. "I fear I misrepresented my riding abilities. Or rather, I failed to mention my complete lack thereof."

His expression softens slightly. "Let us dismount for a moment."

"There's a stream just ahead where the horses can drink," I provide, adjusting my skirts over my ankles.

He guides us to a small clearing where a brook bubbles merrily over smooth stones. In one fluid motion, he dismounts and approaches my side. His hands encircle my waist again, lifting me down as though I weigh nothing at all. For one dizzying moment, I am suspended in his grip, my face level with his. I notice the flecks of amber in his brown eyes, the slight cleft in his chin usually hidden by his perfectly tied cravat.

My feet touch the ground, but his hands linger at my waist a heartbeat longer than necessary. I step back, my legs unsteady beneath me.

"Thank you," I murmur, unable to meet his gaze.

"The pleasure is mine." He secures both horses to a nearby low branch, where they can reach the water.

An uncomfortable silence falls between us. I have no notion how to proceed, what topics might interest him, what cleverness I might offer. My sisters would know exactly what to say, how to charm and engage. I fidget with my gloves, wishing desperately for their social ease.

"You are quiet today," he observes, breaking the silence. "I find myself curious about your thoughts."

"My thoughts are rarely of interest to others," I admit, forcing myself to look at him. "I have little practice in... conversation with gentlemen."

"Then allow me to ease your burden." His smile is unexpected, transforming his solemn features. "I find myself capable of filling silences when necessary."

He proceeds to describe the boundaries of his estate, pointing out landmarks I can only imagine. I listen, grateful for his consideration, watching the animation in his face as he speaks of the land he clearly loves.

When he pauses, I gather my courage to ask: "Why me?"

His eyebrows lift slightly. "I beg your pardon?"

"Forgive my bluntness, but why have you chosen me? There are countless young ladies of appropriate birth and fortune. Many of them beautiful, accomplished, charming."

"Perhaps I prefer sincerity to charm." His expression becomes inscrutable again. "Lady Eleanor, I believe we could suit each other well. I require a duchess who will approach her role with intelligence and dignity. You require—"

"A husband," I finish softly. "Any husband, according to my father."

A shadow crosses his face. "Your father underestimates you."

"Most people do."

He studies me for a long moment before speaking again. "Lady Eleanor Hartwood, would you do me the honor of becoming my wife?"

The words, though expected, still land like stones in still water, sending ripples of shock through me. This is happening. The Duke of Westmoreland is actually proposing marriage to me.

I ought to feel elated. Triumph. Relief at the very least. Instead, uncertainty washes over me. *Does he truly see me, or merely a convenient solution to his need for a duchess?*

I ought to say no—to gather my skirts and flee from this grass, this proposal, this man as swiftly as my feet would carry me. But before I can master my racing thoughts, I hear my own voice speaking as if from a great distance.

"Yes."

The word hangs between us, simple yet irrevocable. I search his face for some flicker of emotion—relief, perhaps, or satisfaction at having secured his practical arrangement. But the Duke's expression remains a study in reserve, his dark eyes revealing nothing of the thoughts moving behind them. *What calculations are running through that handsome head? Does he already regret his choice, finding me wanting even as a convenient solution? Or is this merely the nature of our bargain—a bloodless, practical union devoid of sentiment?*

I press my hands together to still their trembling, wondering what I have just committed myself to.

CHAPTER TEN
NO DISHONOR
THE DUKE OF WESTMORELAND

"I haven't ridden since I was twelve." Her cheeks flush a delightful shade of pink as she speaks, though her gaze remains firmly fixed on the ground between us.

"Twelve?" I cannot hide my astonishment. Most young ladies of quality ride daily.

"Father said I sat a horse like a sack of potatoes. He forbade me from riding thereafter, claiming I would disgrace the family name should anyone witness such an atrocity." Her voice drops to nearly a whisper.

A curious sensation takes hold in my chest—something between anger and protectiveness. *What manner of father would speak thus to his daughter?*

Her steps are measured, careful, as though she fears a misstep might provoke disappointment. I adjust my pace to accommodate her, observing how she carries herself—shoulders slightly hunched, head bowed. She has been taught to make herself small, invisible. *Why does this realization provoke such irritation within me?*

The path narrows as we enter the wood, forcing us to walk closer together. I feel a subtle tensing of her arm against mine.

"I have given some thought to our arrangement," I begin, breaking the silence that has stretched between us. "It would be prudent for us to be seen together publicly before the banns are called."

"Publicly?" Her voice catches on the word.

"Indeed. Would you do me the honor of accompanying me to dinner tomorrow evening at Radley Hall? Lady Radley is hosting a small gathering. Nothing grand, merely twenty or thirty guests."

She stops abruptly, her face draining of color. "Twenty or thirty?"

"Is that a problem?" I study her reaction with growing curiosity.

"I—that is—everyone will stare." Her breath quickens, her chest rising and falling in swift, shallow movements. "They will wonder why you have chosen me. They will look for flaws in my appearance, in my conversation. They will whisper behind their fans about how the great Duke of Westmoreland has settled for plain, awkward Eleanor Hartwood."

I observe the panic rising within her with fascination. Not the calculated vapors often deployed by society women to manipulate men into comfort or concession, but genuine, unadulterated fear.

"By the time we attend, my steward will have already seen to the banns being posted. People will indeed talk, but they will speak of our engagement." I attempt reassurance, but her eyes grow wider still.

"Engagement? So soon?" She takes a step backward, then another, her gaze darting about like that of a trapped animal. "I cannot—I should return—"

In an instant, I recognize her intent to flee. My hand shoots out, grasping her wrist firmly but not painfully. She gasps as I draw her back, guiding her until her back meets the broad trunk of an ancient oak. Not forcibly, but with unmistakable purpose.

"Lady Eleanor." I position myself before her, one hand braced against the tree beside her head, effectively preventing escape without actually touching her beyond my grasp on her wrist. "Breathe."

Her eyes, those unremarkable hazel eyes I had scarcely noticed at first meeting, now appear flecked with gold in the dappled sunlight filtering through the leaves. They fix upon my face with an intensity that suggests she is seeing her doom personified.

"In through your nose," I instruct, demonstrating the action. "Out through your mouth."

To my surprise, she complies, her gaze never leaving mine. One breath, then another. Gradually, the wild fluttering of her pulse beneath my fingertips steadies.

"Better?"

She nods, a small, jerky movement.

"I have no intention of parading you about like a prized mare at Tattersalls," I inform her, loosening my grip on her wrist but maintaining our proximity. "We are to be married. It would appear peculiar if we avoided society entirely."

"I understand." Her voice emerges stronger now, though still soft. "Forgive my unseemly display."

I find myself studying her features more closely than before. The slight tremble of her lower lip. The way her lashes—quite long, actually—sweep down to shield her expression. The delicate arch of her throat as she swallows nervously.

An impulse strikes me—not entirely gentlemanly, I confess. *What might lie beneath that careful composure? Is there passion buried beneath the timidity?*

I lean closer, noting how her breath catches. "Do I frighten you so terribly, Lady Eleanor?"

"Not frighten, precisely," she whispers. "Overwhelm, perhaps."

Her honesty surprises me. I allow my gaze to drift deliberately to her mouth. "And if I were to overwhelm you further?" I murmur, my voice dropping to a register I typically reserve for far different circumstances. "What then?"

A flush spreads across her cheeks, down her throat, disappearing beneath the modest neckline of her riding habit. Her pupils dilate visibly.

"I—I don't know what you mean, Your Grace."

But her body speaks more truthfully than her words. The quickening of her breath. The unconscious parting of her lips. The slight, almost imperceptible swaying toward me rather than away.

Not merely a wallflower, then. A carefully banked fire.

How interesting.

"Perhaps we shall discover the answer together," I suggest, straightening to restore a proper distance between us. "Beginning with dinner tomorrow night. Shall we say seven o'clock? I will send my carriage."

I arrive precisely at seven o'clock at Ravensbrook Hall, as promised. My valet spent an inordinate amount of time ensuring my evening attire was immaculate—a fact that prompted a knowing smirk from my sister when I departed Waltham Manor. I dismissed her implication with a wave of my hand. This is a business arrangement, nothing more, regardless of that curious moment in the woods yesterday.

The elderly butler admits me with a formal bow that speaks of decades of service. "His Lordship requests your presence in his study while Lady Eleanor completes her preparations, Your Grace."

I follow him through the imposing entry hall, my footsteps echoing against marble floors. The house possesses a certain dignity, though it lacks the grandeur of my own ancestral seat.

I find Lord Hartwood standing before a modest fire, a glass of amber liquid in his hand.

"Westmoreland!" He turns with exaggerated joviality. "Brandy?"

"Thank you, no." I remain standing despite his gesture toward a chair. "I trust Lady Eleanor will be down shortly?"

"Women and their toilettes." He chuckles, draining his glass. "Never understood why it takes them hours to accomplish what we manage in minutes."

I offer a noncommittal smile, noting the slight slur in his words. Not his first drink this evening, I suspect.

"Sit, sit. There's a matter we should discuss while we have a moment of privacy." He lowers himself into a worn leather chair, immediately refilling his glass from a crystal decanter.

I perch on the edge of a nearby chair, making no effort to disguise my impatience.

"Eleanor's dowry," he announces with sudden businesslike bluntness. "Quite substantial, I assure you. Thirty thousand pounds—to be paid immediately following the wedding, of course."

"The financial arrangements have already been settled between our solicitors," I remind him, uncomfortable with his mercantile approach to his daughter's future.

"Yes, yes." He waves his hand dismissively. "But I wanted to assure you personally. You're making—" He pauses, his eyes narrowing slightly. "Well, let us speak frankly. My Eleanor is not her sisters. She lacks their beauty, their vivacity. Their charm." Each word falls like a stone. "Are you quite certain about this match? There would be no dishonor in reconsidering."

Something hot and unfamiliar surges through my chest. "No dishonor?" I repeat, my voice dangerously quiet.

"Come now, Westmoreland. You're no green boy. You've had the pick of London's finest for years. Eleanor is..." He searches for a word, settling on, "serviceable. She'll manage your household well enough, I suppose. Bear your children. But surely a man of your standing expected more."

I stand abruptly, my hands clenching at my sides. "I find it curious, Lord Hartwood, that you speak so dismissively of your own daughter."

"Merely being practical." He blinks, seemingly bewildered by my response. "No sense pretending she's something she's not."

"What she is," I state coldly, "is my future Duchess. Her standing will soon eclipse your own. I suggest you consider that carefully before you speak of her in such terms again."

His mouth opens, then closes without sound, resembling nothing so much as a fish suddenly finding itself on dry land.

"Furthermore," I continue, unable to halt the words now flowing like ice water, "I wonder if you have considered that perhaps Lady Eleanor appears diminished in your eyes precisely because you have spent years ensuring she believes herself to be so?"

A flush creeps up his neck. "Now see here—"

"No, I believe I have seen quite enough." I straighten my already impeccable cuffs. "We shall marry in a fortnight. I suggest you accustom yourself to addressing your daughter with the respect her future position demands."

I turn on my heel and stride from the room without awaiting dismissal, my blood still running hot with an anger I scarcely recognize. *What manner of father treats his own child thus?* No wonder Eleanor can barely meet my gaze or speak above a whisper.

My thoughts halt abruptly as I enter the drawing room and find her waiting. She stands beside the window, her slim figure silhouetted against the evening light. At the sound of my entrance, she turns, and for a moment, I cannot speak.

She wears a gown of palest pink, a shade that brings a warmth to her complexion I had not noticed before. Her dark hair is arranged in a deceptively simple style, a few artful tendrils framing her face. The modesty of her appearance holds an understated elegance that strikes me more forcefully than any elaborate artifice.

"Your Grace," she curtsies, her eyes meeting mine briefly before darting away. "I apologize for keeping you waiting."

I cross to her side in four swift strides. "You look..." I search for an appropriate word, settling on, "lovely."

Her eyes widen slightly, disbelief evident in her expression.

"Shall we?" I offer my arm, eager to remove her from this

NO DISHONOR

house, from the influence of a man who cannot see the worth of what stands before him.

She retrieves a delicate pelisse from a nearby chair, and I assist her with it, noting how she startles at my touch upon her shoulders. We move through the hallway with unnecessary haste, my hand at the small of her back guiding her toward the front entrance.

"Your father and I have spoken," I inform her as we approach my waiting carriage. "We are to be married in a fortnight."

"A fortnight?" she whispers, pausing at the carriage door. "So soon?"

"Too soon?" I search her face for signs of distress.

She takes a breath, straightening her shoulders in a gesture of surprising resolution. "No. Not too soon."

"Good." I hand her up into the carriage with perhaps more care than strictly necessary. "Then it is settled."

I cannot tear my gaze from Eleanor as she sits across from me in the carriage. The pale pink of her gown casts a subtle glow upon her features, softening what I had initially dismissed as unremarkable. In the gentle sway of the carriage lanterns, I notice delicate pink pins nestled within her dark hair, glinting like tiny jewels whenever she moves. I find myself smiling inwardly at this small, feminine touch—a detail I would have overlooked mere days ago. After we are wed, I shall ensure she has gowns in every shade of pink imaginable. The color suits her remarkably well.

My thoughts drift to my encounter with Lord Hartwood, that loathsome exchange still burning in my mind. How could a father speak so dismissively of his own child? Even my own father, demanding and exacting as he was, never spoke of Anne or myself with such casual cruelty.

The silence between us stretches uncomfortably. Eleanor sits perfectly still, her hands folded in her lap, her gaze fixed somewhere beyond the carriage window. She seems to have perfected the art of taking up as little space as possible, both physically and otherwise. I find this unaccountably irritating.

"Your father," I say abruptly, causing her to start slightly, "is he always such a contemptible man?"

Her eyes widen at my directness. For a moment, I fear I have overstepped—after all, most daughters maintain at least a pretense of filial devotion no matter how undeserving the parent.

"I—" She falters, then draws a steadying breath. "He has never been particularly... kind... toward me."

"Kind?" I repeat with more force than intended. "The man speaks of you as though you were merchandise he fears might be returned for defects. It is beyond abominable."

A small crease appears between her brows. "You spoke with him about me?"

"He seemed determined to ensure I understood what a grievous disappointment you are," I say, then immediately regret my bluntness when her face pales. "His assessment, not mine," I add hastily.

She smooths her gloves, a nervous gesture I've noticed she employs when uncomfortable. "You need not concern yourself, Your Grace. I am accustomed to his manner."

"That you are accustomed to it makes it no less reprehensible." I lean forward slightly, struck by a sudden desire to see her eyes meet mine directly, without that cursed downward cast. "Tell me, Lady Eleanor—has he always treated you thus?"

For a fleeting moment, she looks directly at me, and I glimpse something in her expression—not merely resignation, but a profound weariness that speaks of years enduring what no daughter should.

"I have never known him to be different," she admits quietly. "With me, at least. My sisters..." She trails off, her gaze returning to the passing darkness outside the window.

"Your sisters were favored," I finish for her.

She nods almost imperceptibly. "Victoria and Elizabeth were blessed with my mother's beauty. They secured brilliant matches with minimal effort. Victoria was barely seventeen when she received three proposals in a single Season." A whisper of a smile touches her lips, but holds no joy. "Father says I exhausted his patience and his pocketbook by requiring five Seasons without result."

My jaw tightens involuntarily. "And yet here you are, engaged to a Duke. One might think that would satisfy even his lofty expectations."

"I believe he finds the situation... puzzling," she murmurs.

"Puzzling?" I echo, feeling my temper rise again.

"He cannot fathom why you would choose me," she explains matter-of-factly, as though discussing the weather rather than her own father's cruel assessment of her worth. "In truth, neither can I."

The simplicity of her statement strikes me more forcefully than any dramatic declaration could have done. She genuinely cannot comprehend why any man of consequence would choose her. *What manner of upbringing creates such certainty of one's own insignificance?*

"Perhaps," I suggest with deliberate lightness, "I possess greater discernment than your esteemed father."

She glances up, surprised by my tone. For an instant—so brief I might have imagined it—a flicker of genuine amusement crosses her features. It transforms her face entirely, hinting at a spirited nature buried beneath layers of carefully cultivated meekness.

"I shall have to remedy this situation," I announce, impulsively reaching across to take her gloved hand in mine. She flinches slightly at the contact but does not withdraw. "When you are my duchess, none shall dare speak to you with anything less than the utmost respect."

Her fingers tremble slightly within my grasp. "You need not trouble yourself on my account, Your Grace."

"Sebastian," I correct her. "If we are to be married in a fortnight, perhaps you might call me by my given name when we are private."

"Sebastian," she repeats, the word sounding strange and tentative on her lips.

I find myself unexpectedly pleased by the sound of my name in her soft voice. "Lady Eleanor—"

"Eleanor," she interjects with surprising assertiveness. "If I am to call you Sebastian, then..."

"Eleanor," I agree, still holding her hand. "A fresh beginning, then. No more living beneath your father's shadow."

She does not respond, but I feel a subtle change in her posture—a straightening of her shoulders, an almost imperceptible lifting of her chin. Perhaps there is more steel in her spine than her father—or indeed, than I—initially recognized.

The carriage slows as we approach Radley Hall, its windows ablaze with light. I release her hand reluctantly, struck by a curious reluctance to relinquish this moment of private understanding between us.

"Shall we brave the lions' den?" I ask, offering a conspiratorial smile.

For the briefest moment, she returns it—a genuine smile that reaches her eyes and transforms her entire countenance. In that instant, I glimpse a woman I have not yet met, but find myself increasingly curious to know.

CHAPTER ELEVEN
SERAPHINA
LADY ELEANOR HARTWOOD

I stand frozen in this opulent drawing room, Sebastian's steady hand at the small of my back the only thing anchoring me to reality. My heart beats a wild, tumultuous rhythm that I fear everyone must hear. Never before have I experienced this peculiar mix of terror and hopefulness. Just moments ago, as we stood on Lady Radley's ornate threshold, I had allowed myself the briefest glimpse of what might be—a future with this enigmatic man, a life built not perhaps on passion, but on something more enduring: mutual respect, shared purpose, maybe even companionship.

"Your Grace! Lady Eleanor!" Lady Radley's voice cuts through my reverie as she hurries toward us, her elaborate turquoise turban bobbing precariously. "What an unexpected pleasure. Had I known you would grace us with your presence this evening, I would have—" She flutters her hands expressively, her eyes darting between us with undisguised curiosity.

Sebastian inclines his head with that effortless grace that

seems so intrinsic to him. "Lady Radley, forgive our intrusion. I wished to introduce society to my future duchess."

Lady Radley's painted eyebrows shoot upward. "Future duchess? Surely not!" She lets out a twitter of nervous laughter that sets my teeth on edge. "There was simply no time—"

"No time?" Sebastian's voice remains pleasant, but I feel his fingers stiffen against my back.

"For a proper courtship," Lady Radley rushes to explain, her cheeks flushing beneath their rouge. "The Season has barely begun and—" She stops, seeming to register the coolness in Sebastian's expression. "Though of course, your affairs are entirely your own, Your Grace."

"Indeed they are," Sebastian replies, the corner of his mouth twitching in what might be amusement or irritation.

"It's just—well—" Lady Radley squirms visibly, looking desperately around at her assembled guests, who have fallen into a hush at our arrival. "There was simply no announcement—"

"I believe the banns will serve as announcement enough," Sebastian interrupts smoothly. His confidence radiates outward like heat from a fire, and I find myself standing straighter beside him.

"And so many believed—that is to say—" Lady Radley's third excuse withers on her lips as heads turn and bodies step aside, creating a pathway through the crowded room.

Time stops. My lungs refuse to draw breath. At the end of this impromptu corridor stands a vision—there is truly no other word for her—of such exquisite beauty that I feel myself diminish by mere proximity.

Miss Seraphina Ashworth moves toward us with the fluid grace of a dancer, each step deliberate and perfectly calculated. The candlelight catches the rich chocolate brown of her upswept hair, shot through with hints of auburn that seem to glow from within. Her gown, a rich sapphire blue silk that must have cost a small fortune, clings to a figure that makes me acutely conscious of my own inadequacies. The low neckline reveals alabaster skin that seems to emit its own pearlescent light.

But it is her eyes that truly capture me—wide-set, almond-shaped, and the precise blue of a summer sky. They sparkle with intelligence and something else—a calculation, perhaps—that feels at odds with the soft smile playing about her perfectly shaped lips.

She glides toward us without awaiting an introduction, her focus entirely on Sebastian. My presence might as well be that of a potted plant for all the acknowledgment she gives me.

"Sebastian," she breathes his name like a prayer, her voice musical and low. "How wonderful to see you again."

I feel Sebastian's entire body tense beside me. The warmth of his hand at my back vanishes as he drops his arm to his side, and suddenly I am adrift, untethered in this sea of curious faces.

"Miss Ashworth," he says, his voice clipped and formal where hers had been intimate.

Only now does she deign to notice me, her gaze flicking over my person with such swift assessment that I feel instantly cataloged and dismissed. I am painfully aware of my unremarkable gown—the pale pink that my mother insisted brought out my eyes but which now seems drab and matronly compared to Miss Ashworth's splendor. My hair, arranged by Wallace with such care, feels lopsided and uninspired.

"Won't you introduce me to your companion?" she asks Sebastian, though her tone suggests she can hardly imagine why he would bother.

Something shifts in Sebastian's demeanor. He stiffens, draws himself up to his full imposing height, and to my utter astonishment, reaches for my hand. His fingers close around mine, warm and firm.

"Miss Ashworth, may I present Lady Eleanor Hartwood," he says, his voice ringing clear in the hushed room. "My fiancée."

The word falls between us like a gauntlet thrown. Miss Ashworth's perfect composure falters for just an instant—a tightening around her eyes, a slight narrowing of her gaze—before she recovers with remarkable speed.

"Your fiancée?" She tilts her head, her smile widening to reveal teeth as white and perfect as pearls. "How utterly... unexpected."

She extends her hand to me with exquisite politeness, but her eyes—those startling blue eyes—are cold and assessing. I feel measured against some standard I cannot hope to meet, cataloged and filed away as no threat whatsoever.

"Lady Eleanor," she says, her voice dripping honey, "what a pleasure to make your acquaintance. Sebastian and I are such dear old friends. I'm certain we shall become great friends as well."

I take her proffered hand, mine trembling slightly within Sebastian's grasp. Her skin is cool and smooth, her grip delicate but somehow viselike. I am suddenly, painfully aware of my own ordinariness, of the vast gulf between her extraordinary beauty and my unremarkable self. Next to this dazzling creature, I am indeed nothing but a shadow, easy to overlook, easier still to forget.

I stand frozen, watching as Sebastian—my fiancé—is led away by the most beautiful woman I have ever seen. Miss Ashworth's hand rests possessively on his sleeve, her face tilted up toward his with practiced intimacy. She says something too low for me to hear, and though Sebastian's expression remains impassive, he doesn't pull away. They move together through the crowd, which parts before them as if acknowledging the rightness of their pairing.

They look perfect together. As if fashioned by the same hand, designed to complement one another. His dark handsomeness alongside her delicate beauty. The whispers have already begun, rustling through the room like wind through autumn leaves.

"I thought she was in mourning still..."

"Did you see the way he looked at her?"

"Lady Eleanor? Who is Lady Eleanor?"

I become aware of my own arms, hanging useless at my sides, and the burning sensation in my lungs that reminds me to breathe. I force air into my chest, though it feels thick and insufficient.

"My dear Lady Eleanor," Lady Radley materializes at my elbow, her face a mask of concern so exaggerated it would be comical under different circumstances. "I simply must apologize."

I blink at her, trying to focus. "Apologize?"

"Had I known about your engagement—" She presses a hand to her considerable bosom. "I would never have invited Miss Ashworth. You must believe me."

"I see no reason for apology," I manage, though my voice sounds distant to my own ears. "You could not have known."

"Well, yes, therein lies the problem." Lady Radley's eyes gleam with barely suppressed excitement. She leans closer, her breath sweet with wine and heavy with some cloying perfume. "No one knew. Such a private courtship! And so... unexpected."

The word stings, echoing Miss Ashworth's assessment of me. Unexpected. Impossible to anticipate or predict. A shock. An anomaly.

"I suppose," Lady Radley continues, lowering her voice to a dramatic whisper that nonetheless carries perfectly, "we all assumed when the Duke finally decided to marry, it would be to... well..." She trails off, but her expressive eyebrows complete the sentence more eloquently than words could. Someone else. Anyone else.

"I understand," I say, fighting to keep my voice level. I want desperately to flee, to hide, but I force myself to remain standing straight, chin lifted. "We have kept our arrangement private."

"Such a tragedy," Lady Radley sighs, though her eyes are alight with the pleasure of sharing a particularly juicy morsel of gossip. "They were to be married, you know. Everything arranged, the church filled with flowers, the most exclusive guest list in London. And then—" She snaps her fingers. "She left him at the altar for the Marquess of Landry. Richer, you see."

Each word strikes like a physical blow. I picture Sebastian waiting, resplendent in his formal attire, watching the church door, minute by agonizing minute, as realization dawns...

"The poor Duke was devastated," Lady Radley continues, oblivious to my distress. "Wouldn't leave Waltham Manor for months afterward. Some said he would never recover."

She glances significantly toward Sebastian and Miss Ashworth, now deep in conversation across the room. "Though seeing them now... well, old passions die hard, do they not?"

Her voice lowers further still, forcing me to lean in despite myself.

"Between us, my dear, I cannot help but wonder if this hasty engagement might be related to that dreadful cousin of his.

The one who will inherit if the Duke doesn't produce an heir soon. Horrid man, always at the gaming tables. It would be a shame to see Waltham Manor in such hands."

The final blow lands with cruel precision. Of course. Sebastian needs a wife—*any wife*—to secure his inheritance. A practical arrangement, as he called it. *What better choice than a plain, grateful nobody who would make no demands of his heart?*

"Excuse me," I whisper, my composure finally shattering. "I find I need some air."

Before Lady Radley can respond, I gather my skirts and flee. I have no destination in mind beyond escape, away from curious eyes and pitying glances. Tears blur my vision as I hurry down a corridor, trying door handles until one gives way. I slip inside what appears to be a small study, mercifully empty, and collapse into a corner chair.

The tears come in earnest now, hot and relentless. I curl into myself, drawing my knees up beneath my skirts in a most unladylike posture, pressing my face against the damask upholstery to muffle my sobs.

How foolish I have been. How painfully, absurdly naive. Did I truly believe, even for a moment, that a man like Sebastian might... what? Come to care for me? See beyond my unremarkable exterior to whatever lies beneath?

The evidence stands before me, clear as cut crystal: the way his entire body tensed at the sight of Miss Ashworth, the haunted look that crossed his features before he mastered himself. Whatever happened between them, his feelings remain unresolved. One does not react so powerfully to someone who means nothing.

I knew this would happen. Have I not witnessed it my entire life? The moment any true beauty appears, I become invisible. A shadow easily overlooked, easily forgotten. It is the natural order of things, and I was a fool to imagine it might be otherwise, even for a moment.

My heart constricts painfully in my chest. The sensation startles me with its intensity. *Why should I feel such acute distress?* This was never to be a love match. Sebastian made that abundantly clear from the outset. A practical arrangement. Mutual benefit. Nothing more.

And yet...

The realization dawns with the force of a physical blow. Somehow, without my noticing or consent, I have fallen in love with the Duke of Westmoreland. Love, that most impractical, inconvenient emotion. Love, which requires reciprocation to bring joy rather than pain. Love, which I am singularly ill-equipped to inspire in anyone, let alone a man accustomed to women of Miss Ashworth's caliber.

The door opens without warning. I jerk upright, hastily wiping at my tear-streaked face. Sebastian stands in the doorway, his tall figure silhouetted against the light from the corridor.

"For what reason are you sequestering yourself?" he inquires, moving into the chamber and shutting the door in his wake. The space seems suddenly diminished by his commanding presence. "And what has caused these tears?"

I remain silent, unable to form words around the knot of emotion lodged in my throat.

I wipe hastily at my face, searching desperately for a plausible explanation. "I felt suddenly ill," I stammer, not meeting his eyes. "The heat of the room was... overwhelming."

The lie sounds hollow even to my own ears. I cannot bring myself to admit the truth—that I fled from the sight of him with Miss Ashworth, that Lady Radley's words cut me to the quick, that I have committed the gravest error a woman in my position could make: developing tender feelings where none are required nor desired.

"The heat of the room," Sebastian repeats, his voice dangerously soft. He strides toward me, his tall frame casting a shadow over my huddled form. "And I suppose the tears streaming down your face are merely a symptom of this sudden illness?"

I lower my eyes, studying the intricate pattern of the carpet. A coward's response, but I have no courage left. "Yes. That is... I mean..."

"Stop. This. Nonsense." Each word falls like a stone between us. He reaches down, his fingers circling my wrist, and pulls me upright with such sudden force that I gasp. I find myself standing far too close to him, close enough to see the pulse beating in his throat above his perfectly tied cravat, close enough to smell the blend of sandalwood and something distinctly him.

The warmth drains from his voice as his obsidian gaze bores into mine, probing with a scrutiny that makes me shift uneasily beneath his stare. "No harm has befallen you at anyone's hand," he declares with unwavering certainty. "I have caused you no wound, no distress."

I try to step back, but his grip on my wrist prevents retreat. "I never suggested—"

His words lash out, demanding, "Then why flee? Why conceal yourself in nooks, tears streaming like an infant?" Vexation colors each utterance as his tone heightens. "If we are to wed, Lady Eleanor, you must exhibit fortitude. Else, females akin to Miss Ashworth shall trample you mercilessly."

His mention of her name sends a fresh stab of pain through my chest. So he recognizes it too—her power, her ability to diminish others simply by existing.

Eleanor's heart thrums as she attempts to extricate herself from his unyielding hold, her voice barely carrying across the space between them. "I confess I cannot comprehend your meaning," she murmurs with unconvincing nonchalance, giving a gentle yet determined pull against his fingers that encircle her wrist like an iron manacle.

He maintains his position unwaveringly. "Feign not ignorance. I observed your exchange with her. She dispatched you with merely a look, and you submitted without resistance."

"What would you have me do?" I ask, a hint of genuine curiosity breaking through my misery. "Challenge her to a duel? Tear at her hair like fishwives at market?"

A flicker of surprise crosses his features, quickly replaced by something more calculating. "So there is some fire in you after all."

"I simply see no purpose in engaging in battles I cannot win," I reply, my voice steadier now. "Miss Ashworth is... unparalleled. I would only embarrass myself and, by extension, you."

His mouth tightens into a hard line. "That is precisely the attitude that ensures defeat before the contest has even begun."

I finally wrench my wrist free, rubbing the skin where his fingers left their mark. "There is no contest, Your Grace. I harbor no illusions about my standing in comparison to a woman like Miss Ashworth."

"And yet I have chosen you as my future duchess," he counters.

A brittle laugh escapes me before I can prevent it. "For entirely practical reasons, as you yourself explained. Not because I can hold my own in society. Not because I inspire admiration or even notice from others."

"So that's it," he says, something like understanding dawning in his expression. "Lady Radley cornered you."

I feel my face heat with embarrassment. "She merely confirmed what I already knew."

"Which was?"

"That our engagement is unexpected. That no one can fathom why you would choose someone like me when you once had someone like her." The words hurt to speak aloud, each one a tiny shard of glass in my throat.

"Someone like you," he repeats slowly. "And what exactly do you believe that to be, Lady Eleanor?"

"Ordinary," I whisper, the truth of it sitting heavy on my chest. "Unremarkable. Invisible."

His countenance clouds over. "You diminish your own worth far too readily."

"And you give me too much," I counter quietly.

Sebastian studies me for a long moment, his gaze so intense I finally have to look away. "Since you are so ill,'" he says at last, "we will leave at once."

Despite everything, I feel a flicker of dismay. "But you wished to stay. I saw your face when Miss Ashworth approached." I hate myself for the weakness in my voice, for caring at all what he does or whom he spends time with. "You need not leave on my account."

Sebastian's face hardens as he weighs his options, his expression becoming a perfect mask of aristocratic indifference. "I believe I will stay after all," he says, each word precise and devoid of emotion. "I shall make your excuses to our hosts. The carriage will see you safely home."

I feel something crumble inside me, a fragile hope I hadn't even realized I was harboring. His demeanor is so cold, so utterly devoid of warmth that I can barely breathe through the ache in my chest. The arrogant tilt of his chin, the dismissive flick of his wrist as he signals for a footman—these are the gestures of a man who has had quite enough of an inconvenient obligation.

"Of course," I manage, my voice barely audible even to my own ears. "Thank you for your... consideration."

I catch the briefest flicker of his gaze toward where Miss Ashworth stands surrounded by admirers, her laughter like crystal bells across the room. Of course, he would choose her company over mine. *What man wouldn't?* I lower my eyes, unwilling to let him see how deeply his casual dismissal wounds me.

CHAPTER TWELVE
ENTANGLEMENT
THE DUKE OF WESTMORELAND

I watch Eleanor's carriage disappear down the drive, the white handkerchief she held fluttering from the window like a pathetic surrender flag. The sight of it—of her fleeing the gathering because of Seraphina's appearance—ignites a fury so potent within me that I barely recognize myself.

My chest heaves as I turn back toward the house, boots crunching angrily against the gravel. Blood pounds in my ears, drowning out the chirping of evening birds and distant laughter from Lady Radley's guests. The drawing room's warmth and chatter hit me like a physical blow as I re-enter. I do not pause to acknowledge the curious glances thrown my way but stride directly toward the drinking room.

"Brandy," I demand of the footman. "A double."

The servant pours with the practiced precision of one accustomed to attending gentlemen in various states of agitation. I do not thank him, merely seize the glass and drain half in a single swallow. The liquor burns a welcome path down my throat.

From this vantage point, I have an unimpeded view of Seraphina. She stands amidst a circle of admirers, her dark curls gleaming in the chandelier light, her blue gown cut scandalously low. A calculated design, no doubt. I observe how she tosses her head back in practiced laughter at something Lord Hastings says, how her gloved hand lingers on his sleeve.

I recognize every mannerism, every calculated gesture. They were once directed at me.

What a fool I was.

I finish my brandy and set the glass down with more force than necessary. Several heads turn. Good. Let them look. Let them speculate. I care not what society whispers about me tonight.

Eleanor's face flashes before me—the hurt in her eyes, the quiet dignity with which she accepted my suggestion to return home. "I shall not be in your way," she had said. As if she were the interloper and not Seraphina.

No. This needs to end tonight. I sent Eleanor away precisely for this purpose—to confront the ghost that has haunted me these three years past. To ensure that when I return to her, there will be no specter of Seraphina between us.

I straighten my cravat, adjust my jacket, and with deliberate steps cross the room to where Seraphina holds court.

"Miss Ashworth," I interrupt whatever trivial conversation flows around her. "Might I have a moment of your time?"

Her eyes widen fractionally—the only genuine reaction she's shown all evening. "Your Grace," she responds, her voice honey-smooth. "Of course."

The gentlemen surrounding her scatter with reluctant murmurs. I offer my arm, which she takes with exaggerated care, her fingers pressing into my sleeve with familiar possessiveness.

I guide her to an alcove near the window—visible to the entire assembly, yet removed enough for private conversation. I position myself so my back is to the wall, facing outward. I will give no gossip fodder tonight.

"Sebastian," she breathes, using my Christian name with calculated intimacy. "How wonderful to see you again after so long."

Her scent remains unchanged—jasmine and something darker. Once, that fragrance dominated my dreams. Now it merely irritates my senses.

"Is it wonderful, Seraphina? I rather thought our last meeting concluded our acquaintance quite definitively."

Her lips form a practiced pout. "You've grown hard, Your Grace."

"And you've grown bold, addressing me with such familiarity."

She steps closer, eyes glittering. "We were once far more than familiar, were we not?"

My body remembers her—that is the devil of it. Remembers the softness of her lips, the warmth of her skin beneath my hands in stolen moments before our wedding was to take place. Remembers entangling my fingers in those dark curls, whispering promises against her neck.

Would she still feel the same? Would her body still arch against mine with that practiced grace? For a treacherous moment, I imagine pulling her into my arms, tasting those lips that once consumed my every thought.

But alongside these memories comes the recollection of standing alone at the altar. The pitying glances. The humiliation. The note delivered by her maid: "I have accepted another's proposal. Forgive me."

No. What she once was to me, she can never be again.

"Why did you leave me at the altar?" I ask plainly, watching her expression shift from seductive to calculating.

"Sebastian," she sighs, eyes downcast. "You must understand my position then. I received another offer—"

"So your note indicated."

"Marquess Landry was most insistent," she continues. "His estate was considerably larger, his connections more prestigious. Surely you understand that a woman must make advantageous choices when they present themselves."

"And yet here you stand, a widow. How unfortunate that your advantageous choice proved so temporary."

A flash of genuine anger crosses her features. "I did not mean to wound you."

I laugh—a harsh sound devoid of humor. "You did not mean to wound me? You abandoned me on our wedding day without so much as a proper conversation. You humiliated me before all of society."

"It was poorly handled," she concedes, recovering her composure. Her hand reaches for mine. "But perhaps fate has granted us another chance. We are both free now—"

I step back, removing myself from her touch. "I am not free. I am engaged to Lady Eleanor Hartwood."

"The plain Hartwood girl?" Seraphina scoffs. "I heard the rumors but could scarcely credit them. Surely you cannot be serious about her."

I feel my jaw tighten. "You would do well to speak of my future duchess with respect."

Seraphina's laugh is musical and mocking. "Your duchess? Sebastian, darling, you cannot possibly intend to go through with it. Everyone knows why you chose her—a convenient match to secure your inheritance before your cousin can claim it. But now that I am available again..."

"Eleanor is not a convenience," I hear myself say, the words emerging before I've fully formed the thought. "She is intelligent, accomplished—"

"She is inadequate," Seraphina interrupts, her perfect lips curled in disdain. "No beauty, no accomplishments, no particular charm in company. What could she possibly offer that I cannot?"

The question hangs between us, and I find myself searching for an answer that will convince her—convince myself—that my choice is sound. Eleanor's face appears in my mind: not the blank mask she presents to society, but the animated countenance I glimpsed when she spoke of music, when she laughed with her nieces and nephews in the garden, grass stains on her skirts and sunshine in her hair.

"She is genuine," I say finally. "She wants nothing from me but what I freely give."

Even as the words leave my mouth, I realize they sound hollow—unconvincing even to my own ears. *What do I truly know of Eleanor's motivations?* We have spent mere days in each other's company. Our engagement is precisely what Seraphina describes: a business arrangement.

Seraphina perceives my uncertainty and presses her advantage, stepping closer. Her familiar scent envelops me. "Sebastian, we both know this is madness. You and I—we understand each other. We move in the same circles, share the same sensibilities."

"We shared nothing but mutual deception," I reply, but my voice lacks conviction.

"Then why did you approach me tonight? Why send your little fiancée home if not to speak to me alone?" Her hand rests on my chest, her blue eyes looking up at me through dark lashes. "You still feel something for me. I know it."

For three years, I have imagined this moment—confronting the woman who humiliated me, who broke my heart, and walked away without a backward glance. In my imagination, I remained cold, unmoved by her beauty, impervious to her charms. The reality is more complex. The wound she inflicted has scabbed over, but not fully healed.

Seraphina mistakes my silence for wavering. She leans closer, her lips a breath away from mine. "Break the engagement, Sebastian. No one would blame you—least of all her. She must know she doesn't deserve you."

Eleanor's tearful face flashes before me—the wounded dignity with which she excused herself from the gathering when Seraphina appeared. The memory stirs something protective within me. No, not protective. *Possessive*. When did I begin to think of her as mine?

"You're wrong," I say, stepping back from Seraphina's embrace. "If anything, I don't deserve her."

Seraphina's expression shifts from seductive to confused. "What are you talking about?"

I shake my head, suddenly weary of this encounter, of Seraphina, of all the emotional entanglements I've spent years avoiding. "It does not matter. I wish you well in your search for a new husband, but it won't be me."

Her beautiful face hardens. "You'll regret this. When the novelty of playing savior to that mousy little creature wears off, you'll remember what it was like between us."

"I remember precisely what it was like between us—which is why I am certain I will never regret my decision." I bow slightly. "Good evening, Miss Ashworth."

I turn away before she can respond, moving through the crowd with purpose. My mind races ahead of me, toward Ravensbrook Hall, toward Eleanor. The image of her tear-streaked face haunts me. Why does her pain disturb me so? I have witnessed countless women cry—theatrical displays designed to manipulate, to extract sympathy or concessions.

But Eleanor's tears were different. Private. Genuine. She tried to hide them from me, turning her face away as she climbed into the carriage. "I shall be perfectly fine, Your Grace," she had insisted, though her voice trembled. "Please enjoy your evening."

It bothers me that she left believing I preferred Seraphina's company to hers. It bothers me more that, until this moment, I wasn't certain she was wrong.

What is Eleanor to me now? No longer merely a means to an end—a convenient bride to secure my inheritance. Yet I cannot name this shifting emotion. Not love, surely. We scarcely know each other. Respect, perhaps. Interest, certainly. *Protection? Possession?*

"Your Grace, you look troubled." Lady Radley materializes before me, her shrewd eyes assessing my expression. "I trust Miss Ashworth's unexpected appearance hasn't disturbed your evening?"

"Not at all," I reply smoothly. "But I find I must take my leave.

Lady Eleanor has returned to Ravensbrook Hall, and I should join her."

Lady Radley's eyebrows rise. "So soon? The night is young."

"I apologize for the abrupt departure, but I have pressing matters to attend to."

Her lips curve in a knowing smile. "Of course. Young love cannot bear separation, can it? Will we receive an invitation to the wedding? I should be most disappointed to miss such a significant occasion."

For the first time this evening, my smile is genuine. "Of course, Lady Radley. I wouldn't dream of excluding you."

She pats my arm. "Excellent. Now go to your bride. A woman should never be left wondering where she stands, especially not on the night she encounters her future husband's former fiancée."

I bow over her hand. "Your wisdom is, as always, impeccable."

As my carriage pulls away from Lady Radley's home, I find my thoughts racing ahead to Ravensbrook Hall, to Eleanor. *I need to see her, to explain... what, exactly? That Seraphina means nothing to me? That our engagement is not merely convenient but... something more?*

The truth is, I don't know what Eleanor has become to me. Only that, for the first time since Seraphina's betrayal, I find myself looking forward rather than back.

CHAPTER THIRTEEN
SPINSTERS
LADY ELEANOR HARTWOOD

I walk along the eastern edge of Ravensbrook's grounds with no destination in mind. The spring sunshine bathes everything in golden light, transforming the rolling Yorkshire countryside into something from a painting. Birds flit between the budding trees, calling to one another in cheerful song. Wildflowers dot the meadow with splashes of yellow and purple.

It is, by any measure, a beautiful day.

Yet I feel nothing but hollowness inside.

Three days. Three entire days have passed since I last saw or heard from the Duke of Westmoreland. My so-called fiancé. The man who swept into my life with a business proposition masquerading as a marriage offer, only to vanish the moment his former love reappeared.

I kick at a stone in my path, watching it tumble down the gentle slope. What a fool I have been. What a ridiculous, romantic fool to imagine, even for a moment, that this arrangement might transform into something genuine. That the way Sebastian looked at me during our ride, the way his hand lingered on mine as he helped me dismount, might signify something beyond polite obligation.

I reach the old oak that marks the boundary between the cultivated gardens and the wilder parkland beyond. Father will be furious when he discovers I have ventured this far unaccompanied, but I cannot bring myself to care. Let him rage. Let him lament the embarrassment of his plain, unwanted daughter being jilted by a duke. It would hardly be the first time I have disappointed him.

The truth settles hard in my chest. There will be no wedding. Sebastian has undoubtedly rekindled his romance with the breathtaking Miss Ashworth. *How could he not?* I saw the way she looked at him that night, the familiar intimacy in how she touched his arm. I saw, too, the way he tensed at her proximity—not with discomfort, but with awareness.

What man, having once possessed such a diamond, would settle for a pebble?

I press on, my walking boots now damp with morning dew as I cross into the meadow beyond the oak. The grass here grows wild and lush, dotted with early primroses. The land slopes upward to form a gentle hill, and without conscious decision, I find myself climbing it.

From the summit, I can see Ravensbrook Hall in the distance, its weathered stone catching the sunlight. How small it looks from here, how insignificant the human affairs conducted within its walls.

I glance around, confirming my solitude. No gardeners or grooms in sight. No one to report back to Father or Victoria about my unladylike behavior. With a sigh that feels drawn from the deepest part of me, I lower myself onto the grass, not caring about grass stains or propriety.

I lie back, staring directly into the vast blue sky above. Clouds drift lazily across its expanse, formless and free in ways I shall never be.

"It is not so terrible," I whisper to myself, "to be alone."

I have managed these twenty-three years, have I not? I can continue as I have been. Perhaps in ten years' time, when the bloom of youth has fully faded from my cheeks and my expectations have appropriately diminished, some elderly gentleman might seek a companion for his declining years. Or a widower with small children might require a mother for his offspring rather than a wife for himself.

There are worse fates than spinsterhood. Loving and not being loved in return, for instance. Yes, far better to remain as I am than to bind myself to someone who would always be looking over my shoulder, searching for a more beautiful woman.

I know a few spinsters—Miss Fairchild who teaches music to the village children, and my father's cousin Agatha who travels abroad each summer. They seem content enough with their lot, these friendly women who fill their days with purpose rather than pining. Miss Fairchild speaks with genuine enthusiasm about her pupils' progress, while Cousin Agatha regales us with tales of Roman ruins and Venetian canals that I could scarcely imagine seeing for myself.

Perhaps spinsterhood need not be the dreary sentence society paints it to be. These women have fashioned lives of quiet dignity, free from the disappointments of an indifferent husband or the pain of unrequited devotion. They answer to no one but themselves. Could it truly be so terrible to chart one's own modest course through life, rather than suffer the exquisite torment of loving someone who regards you with nothing warmer than polite tolerance? At least a spinster might preserve her heart intact, if somewhat unused.

I close my eyes against the brightness of the sun, allowing its warmth to seep into my skin. There is peace in acceptance, I decide. Peace in releasing impossible dreams. Like water cupped in desperate hands, the more tightly one clutches at happiness, the more quickly it seems to drain away. Perhaps contentment lies not in grasping, but in opening one's palms and letting go of expectations that were never meant to be fulfilled. Is that not what my music has taught me—that beauty can be found even in the most melancholy of melodies?

A shadow falls across my face, blocking the sunlight. I squint upward, momentarily blinded by the contrast.

"Lady Eleanor, I believe this highly irregular position explains why your lady's maid has been frantically searching the grounds for the past hour."

I bolt upright, narrowly avoiding a collision with Sebastian's head as he bends over me. He stands with his feet planted on either side of where I lay, his tall frame backlit by sunshine, making it difficult to read his expression.

"Your Grace!" I scramble to my feet, mortified to be caught in such an undignified pose. Grass clings to my hair and muslin gown, and I brush at it ineffectually. "I did not—that is—I was merely—"

"Communing with nature? Contemplating the philosophical implications of cloud formations? Or perhaps testing alternative methods of landscape appreciation?" His lips quirk upward. "I must say, your approach is most unconventional, though I cannot fault your selection of location. The view is rather magnificent."

Heat blazes across my cheeks. "I did not expect company," I mutter, unable to meet his gaze.

"Evidently." He reaches forward, plucking a blade of grass from my hair with unexpected gentleness. "Though I confess, I find your present dishevelment vastly preferable to the rigid propriety most young ladies maintain. One gets rather tired of perfection."

I blink at him in confusion. "What are you doing here?" The question emerges more bluntly than I intended, but after three days of silence, I cannot muster politeness.

"Looking for you, obviously." He gestures broadly. "Though I expected to find you in the music room or perhaps the library. I did not anticipate needing to launch a full expedition into the wilds of Yorkshire to locate my fiancée."

"Fiancée?" The word catches in my throat. "You still—that is—I assumed after Lady Radley's dinner, and Miss Ashworth's return, that our arrangement was..." I trail off, uncertain how to continue.

Sebastian's expression shifts, something unreadable flashing in his dark eyes.

"Lady Eleanor, did you genuinely believe I would abandon our engagement because a woman who once publicly humiliated me happened to appear at a country dinner party?"

I hurry to my feet, awkwardly attempting to brush the grass stains from the back of my gown. My fingers work frantically at the fabric, knowing full well I'll not be able to rescue it from Wallace's disapproval. The familiar weight of inadequacy settles over me—caught in an undignified position, my appearance compromised, surely disappointing yet another person who expected better.

Sebastian follows my movements with barely concealed amusement, lips twitching as he watches my feeble attempts at restoration.

"You might find it more effective to simply tell your lady's maid you were engaged in critical botanical research," he suggests, eyes twinkling. "I could provide a formal ducal certification of its scientific importance, if necessary."

Despite myself, I feel the corner of my mouth lift slightly. I take a step back, creating a proper distance between us while I gather my scattered composure.

"Your Grace," I begin, my voice steadier than I expected, "I must ask plainly—do you truly still wish to marry me? I would understand completely if recent events have... altered your considerations." I clasp my hands tightly before me, bracing for his answer. "There would be no shame in reconsidering."

Sebastian turns suddenly, pivoting on his heel to face away from me. His broad shoulders rise with a deep breath as he gazes out over the sprawling countryside. The morning sun catches in his dark hair, highlighting strands of chestnut I'd never noticed before.

For several excruciating seconds, he says nothing.

"The thought did cross my mind," he finally admits, his voice carrying clearly despite his averted face. "After you fell suddenly 'ill' and requested to leave the dinner party with such urgent haste."

My cheeks burn. We both know there was no illness.

"You left me there," he continues, something unfamiliar coloring his tone, "alone to face that den of ice and insincere smiles, with Seraphina holding court at its center."

I stare at his back, unsure what response he expects. *An apology? Excuses?*

"I was angry with you," he says more softly, turning just enough that I can glimpse his profile. "Not because you fled—though I confess that stung—but because I wanted..." He pauses, seeming to search for the right words. "I wanted to see you stand up for yourself."

"Stand up for myself?" I repeat, genuinely bewildered.

Sebastian turns fully toward me now, piercing me with that intense gaze that seems to see far more than I wish to reveal.

"Yes. To show the dignity and worth I know lies beneath that carefully constructed invisibility. To demonstrate that women like Seraphina, for all their outward beauty and practiced charm, are the impoverished ones in spirit." His jaw tightens. "Not you."

I blink rapidly, struggling to process his words. "You wanted me to... to what? Make a scene? Challenge her in some way?"

"Not a scene. Simply to exist in your own right—to claim your space without apology." His expression softens marginally. "Instead, you disappeared, leaving the impression that you believed yourself unworthy to stand beside me."

Something unfamiliar stirs within me—not quite anger, but a distant cousin to it. "And you believed punishing me with silence for three days would somehow inspire greater confidence?"

Sebastian has the grace to look momentarily abashed. "That was... poorly handled on my part. I needed time to speak with Seraphina, to ensure certain matters were permanently settled. And then estate business required immediate attention." He steps closer. "But I should have sent word. That was inexcusable."

"Yes, it was," I agree, surprising myself with my forthrightness.

He studies me with renewed interest. "There it is. The one who feels deeply but hides it from the world."

I look away, uncomfortable with his scrutiny. "You still haven't answered my question. Do you wish to continue with our engagement?"

"I do," Sebastian says without hesitation. "Perhaps now more than before."

This catches me entirely off guard. "Why? Surely seeing Miss Ashworth again must have reminded you of what you're sacrificing by settling for—" I stop myself, but the unspoken word hangs between us.

"Settling?" Sebastian's voice takes on a dangerous edge. "Is that what you believe I am doing?"

I lift my chin slightly. 'Is it not? The beautiful Miss Ashworth rejected you, and now you're content with plain, forgettable Lady Eleanor Hartwood because she's convenient and undemanding. A business arrangement, as you said yourself."

"And if I've discovered that perhaps there's more to this arrangement than I initially perceived?"

"Then I would suggest you examine your motivations carefully," I reply, finding courage I didn't know I possessed. "I have no desire to be chosen merely because I represent the safest option for your wounded pride."

Sebastian's eyebrows rise fractionally, and something that might almost be respect flickers in his expression.

"*Ah*...There she is again," he murmurs. "The real Eleanor Hartwood."

"I have always been real," I counter. "Perhaps you simply weren't looking properly."

His lips curve into a genuine smile—not the practiced charm he displays in society, but something rarer and more intriguing.

"Perhaps I wasn't," he concedes. "But I am looking now, Lady Eleanor. And I find myself increasingly interested in what I see."

CHAPTER FOURTEEN
A DAMP CLOTH
LADY ELEANOR HARTWOOD

I take a delicate bite of toast, scarcely tasting it as my mind drifts once more to yesterday's afternoon with Sebastian.

"Eleanor, you shall wear away your fingertips if you continue to touch your lips so," Victoria says with a knowing smile.

I drop my hand immediately, heat rushing to my cheeks. "I was merely checking for crumbs."

"Of course you were," she says, exchanging an amused glance with her husband. "And I suppose those many sighs are simply to clear your lungs of the morning air."

"I do not sigh," I protest, though I feel my lips curve upward without permission.

Even Father's absence from the breakfast table cannot diminish my spirits this morning. Tomorrow I shall be a duchess—not merely any duchess, but Sebastian's duchess.

The very thought makes my heart perform a little dance beneath my ribs.

The door opens rather abruptly, and Father strides in, his boots muddy and his expression harried. His hair stands at odd angles, as though he has repeatedly run his fingers through it in agitation.

"Good morning, Father," I say brightly. "You have missed the most delightful scones."

He barely acknowledges me. "Dreadful business at the McBrides' farm," he announces, dropping heavily into his chair at the head of the table. "Simply dreadful."

Victoria sits up straighter. "What has happened, Father? Not another failed crop?"

"Worse. Illness has gripped the family." He gestures impatiently for coffee. "Those three little ones have been abed with fever for days now, and this morning, McBride himself could not rise from his bed. Delirious with fever, the poor man."

"How terrible," I murmur, genuine concern breaking through my happiness. The McBrides have always been kind to me when I've accompanied Father on his rounds of the estate.

"Terrible indeed," Father says, seizing a piece of toast. "And at the worst possible time. The south field must be plowed within the week or we shall lose the entire planting season there."

"Can Mrs. McBride not nurse them?" my brother-in-law inquires.

A DAMP CLOTH

Father snorts. "The woman is at her wit's end. Cannot manage both the farm and four invalids. She has the constitution of a fieldmouse and twice the nervousness." He takes a large gulp of coffee. "I have sent word to the doctor, but with the influenza spreading through the village, I doubt he will come before tomorrow evening."

"That is most unfortunate," I say, my thoughts already drifting back to the matter of which ribbons I should choose for my hair tomorrow. Perhaps the pale pink that Sebastian seemed to admire when I wore it last—"

"Eleanor could go," Victoria says suddenly.

I blink, pulled from my pleasant reverie. "I beg your pardon?"

Father turns toward me, a considering look in his eyes. "Yes... yes, that might answer."

"What might answer?" I ask, confused.

"You could nurse the McBrides," Victoria continues. "Remember that course you took at Miss Harrington's? Two entire months of nursing instruction that you excelled in."

I stare at my sister in disbelief. "That was five years ago!"

"Knowledge does not simply vanish from one's mind," Father says, warming to the idea with alarming speed. "And you have always had a steady hand and a calm disposition. Perfect for sickroom duties."

"But—but I cannot possibly go today," I protest. "I must prepare for my wedding. Tomorrow, Father. I am to be married tomorrow."

"What preparations remain?" Victoria asks practically. "Your gown is finished. The flowers are ordered. The breakfast is arranged. What could possibly require your attention that cannot wait until this evening?"

I open my mouth, then close it again. In truth, there is little left to do that is not already in capable hands. But to spend my final day as Lady Eleanor Hartwood tending to feverish farmers rather than dreaming of my new life seems unbearably cruel.

"I simply cannot," I say firmly. "Surely there is someone else—"

"Someone else who has been trained in nursing practices?" Father interrupts. "Someone with gentle hands who knows how to prepare medicinal teas and poultices? Someone who will not panic at the first sign of delirium?" He shakes his head. "You know very well our options are limited."

Victoria reaches across the table to take my hand. "Remember when little Mary McBride brought you those wildflowers last spring? And how John McBride carved that little wooden bird for you at Christmas?"

I do remember. The McBrides have always treated me with kindness, never with the dismissive pity I so often encounter elsewhere. Little Mary, with her gap-toothed smile and freckled nose, follows me about like a duckling whenever I visit.

My resistance crumbles. "Very well," I concede. "I shall go, but only for the morning. I must return by afternoon to—" I falter, unable to produce a single truly essential task.

"To continue floating about the house with that dreamy expression?" Victoria teases gently. "I promise your thoughts of the Duke will remain intact, even while you tend to the McBrides."

Father nods approvingly. "That's my girl. I knew you would not disappoint me."

The praise, rare as it is, warms me unexpectedly. "I shall need to gather some supplies," I say, my practical nature asserting itself. "Willow bark for the fever, perhaps some chamomile and honey for the children. And clean linens."

"I shall have Wallace pack a basket immediately," Victoria says, rising from her chair. "And I shall lend you my sturdiest boots. The path to the McBride cottage will be muddy after last night's rain."

As they bustle about making preparations, I realize with some surprise that my joy has not diminished. Tomorrow I shall be Sebastian's duchess, but today I can still be Eleanor Hartwood, who has more to offer than a plain face and a talent for fading into the background. I can be useful.

"I shall be ready to depart within the hour,' I announce, standing straighter. "And I shall do what I can for the McBrides."

I arrive at the McBride farm just as the morning mist begins to lift from the fields. The cottage, usually a place of cheerful activity with children playing in the yard and Mrs. McBride hanging linens on the line, stands eerily quiet. Only the occasional cough breaks the stillness, floating through an open window like a grim herald.

The door creaks as I push it open with my shoulder, basket of supplies balanced against my hip. "Mrs. McBride?" I call softly. "Mr. McBride? It is Lady Eleanor come to help."

No answer greets me. I step inside, the floorboards groaning beneath my borrowed boots. The familiar scent of bread that typically perfumes this humble home has been replaced by something sharper, medicinal—the unmistakable smell of sickness.

I move toward the main room where the children typically gather around the hearth. The sight that greets me turns my blood to ice.

All three McBride children lie sprawled across pallets on the floor, their small bodies shivering despite the blankets heaped upon them. Little Mary's golden curls stick to her forehead, darkened with sweat. Beside her, young Thomas tosses restlessly, his lips cracked and dry. The baby, not yet a year old, whimpers weakly from a makeshift cradle.

Mr. McBride sits slumped in a wooden chair nearby, his breathing labored, his normally ruddy complexion alarmingly pale beneath his beard. His eyes flutter open as I enter, but there is no recognition in their glazed depths.

"Mrs. McBride?" I call again, more urgently now.

A soft moan from the kitchen draws me forward. There on the floor, as though her legs had simply given way beneath her, lies Mrs. McBride. Her apron is twisted around her thin frame, her face flushed with fever.

A violent hissing sound pulls my attention to the fireplace where a pot of water boils furiously, nearly burnt dry, the bottom glowing an alarming red. I rush forward, seizing a thick cloth from my basket to protect my hand as I carefully lift the pot from its hook and set it aside.

There is no time for uncertainty or hesitation. These people need immediate care.

I hurry outside to the well, grateful that Victoria insisted I wear sturdy boots as I navigate the muddy path. The bucket feels impossibly heavy as I haul it back, water sloshing over the sides, but I barely notice the strain. Inside once more, I set to work with a determination that surprises even me.

From my basket, I retrieve the clean linens Victoria provided, tearing them into strips. I dip them in the cool water and move first to the children, placing the damp cloths on their burning foreheads. Their small bodies radiate heat like tiny furnaces.

"There now," I murmur to Mary as she stirs slightly at my touch. "Lady Eleanor is here. You shall be well soon."

I remove their shoes and socks, recalling from my nursing lessons that allowing the feet to remain uncovered helps the body release excess heat. Thomas whimpers as I tug off his woolen socks, but does not wake.

Mr. McBride proves more challenging. He is a large man, broad-shouldered from years of farm labor, and I struggle to remove his heavy boots without disturbing his fitful rest. When at last I succeed, I place a cool cloth on his forehead as well.

Mrs. McBride cannot remain on the kitchen floor. I kneel beside her, slipping one arm beneath her shoulders. "Mrs. McBride," I say firmly, using the voice I once heard a hospital matron employ. "I must help you to your bed."

Her eyes flutter open, confusion evident in their feverish depths. "Lady Eleanor?" she rasps.

"Yes. I am here to help. Can you stand if I support you?"

Together, through a combination of my determination and her momentary lucidity, we manage to make our way to the small bedroom she shares with her husband. Once she is settled on the bed, I place a cool cloth on her brow as well.

Now for the medicines. I set water to boil in a clean pot and prepare the willow bark tea, measuring carefully. While it steeps, I search the kitchen for broth. Finding some in a covered pot, I warm it gently.

Mary proves the easiest to coax into drinking. "Like honey tea at a fancy party," I tell her, and her parched lips curl into the ghost of a smile as she sips.

Thomas requires more persuasion, and the baby takes only a few spoonfuls of the weakened tea before turning away. Mr. McBride drinks mechanically when I hold the cup to his lips, while Mrs. McBride manages a grateful sip before falling back into restless sleep.

Hours pass. I move from one patient to another, replacing cloths as they warm, coaxing sips of tea and broth, speaking gentle nonsense to the children when they stir. My back aches from bending, my hands are raw from wringing cloths, but I do not stop.

I stagger mid-step as I make my way to the fireplace, the room suddenly tilting around me. My hand flies out to steady myself against the mantelpiece, fingers gripping the cool stone. *What was that?* A wave of dizziness washes over me, momentarily blurring my vision. I blink rapidly, willing the sensation away. Perhaps it's merely fatigue catching up with me after these endless hours of tending to the sick. I draw a deep breath and reach for the kettle to heat more water, though my limbs feel oddly heavy, as if weighted with sand. I cannot afford weakness now, not when so many depend upon my care. Straightening my shoulders, I force myself to continue, even as a small voice of warning whispers in the back of my mind.

The shadows have lengthened considerably when a sharp knock at the door announces the doctor's arrival. He sweeps in, medical bag in hand, his expression grave beneath his spectacles.

"Lady Eleanor?" His surprise is evident. "What are you doing here?"

"Tending to the McBrides, Doctor." I stand, wiping my hands on my apron. "They were all ill when I arrived this morning."

He frowns, moving immediately to the nearest child. "How long have you been in this house?"

"Several hours now. I've been giving them willow bark tea and—"

"You must leave immediately." He cuts me off, his voice sharp with alarming urgency. "This is influenza, and a particularly virulent strain. You've been exposed for far too long already."

"But the children—"

"I shall tend to them now. Go, Lady Eleanor. Return home and inform your family of your exposure."

Fear, cold and relentless, grips my heart. I gather my things with trembling hands, glancing back at the children who have come to depend on my care throughout this long day.

"Go," the doctor insists, already turning his attention to little Mary.

Outside, the afternoon air feels unexpectedly cool against my skin. The path home seems longer than it did this morning, winding through fields that blur strangely before my eyes. My limbs feel strangely heavy, as though I wade through water rather than walk on solid ground.

Halfway home, a curious warmth begins to spread through my body. My brow dampens not with exertion but with something else—something I recognize with growing horror from the symptoms I've been treating all day.

The basket slips from my fingers. I reach for it, but my balance fails me. The world tilts alarmingly.

I try to take another step toward home, toward tomorrow, toward Sebastian and our wedding. My legs refuse to obey.

The ground rises to meet me, or perhaps I fall to meet it. The last thing I remember is the cool touch of grass against my burning cheek as darkness claims me.

CHAPTER FIFTEEN
NOT AGAIN
THE DUKE OF WESTMORELAND

I stand at the altar, my fingers absently adjusting cuffs that need no adjustment. The morning sun filters through the stained glass of the small country church, casting kaleidoscope patterns across the floor. For once, a genuine sense of contentment has settled over me—not the false confidence I've crafted for ballrooms, but something unfamiliar and fragile.

"If you continue fiddling with those cuffs, you'll wear holes through them before she arrives," Henry says with that insufferable grin of his. "And here I thought dukes were supposed to be paragons of composure."

"I am perfectly composed," I reply, though my voice sounds strained even to my own ears.

Henry laughs and claps me on the shoulder. "Of course you are. Just as composed as I was when Anne and I wed. I believe I knocked over a vase of flowers and stepped on the vicar's foot within the first five minutes."

Despite myself, I smile. "Yes, well, one must strive to set a higher standard than that."

"There we are!" Henry exclaims. "A smile! I was beginning to fear your face had permanently frozen in that ducal scowl. Lady Eleanor might reconsider if she thinks she's marrying a man incapable of happiness."

The mention of reconsideration sends an unwelcome shiver through me. "That's hardly amusing."

"My apologies," Henry says, his expression softening. "Poor taste on my part. But truly, Sebastian, there's no need for nerves. This isn't—"

"I am aware this isn't the same," I interject, more sharply than intended.

Henry nods, merciful enough not to finish his thought. This isn't like last time. Eleanor isn't Seraphina. I know this, rationally, and yet the memory of standing in a church much grander than this one, waiting for a bride who never appeared, remains uncomfortably vivid.

I distract myself by surveying the gathering. The church fills steadily, pew by pew. Anne sits in the front row, attempting to keep my youngest niece from climbing over the wooden bench while the older two whisper behind their hands. My sister catches my eye and smiles encouragingly.

Relatives and acquaintances filter in—the expected faces of country society, a smattering of London connections who've made the journey north. Mrs. Radley appears, prompting a momentary tensing of my shoulders until I confirm she is blissfully unaccompanied by her recent houseguest.

Something strikes me as the church continues to fill. Not a presence, but an absence.

"Henry," I murmur, "do you see Lord Hartwood or any of Eleanor's sisters?"

Henry scans the gathering, his smile faltering slightly. "Perhaps they're accompanying the bride?"

"Perhaps." The word hangs between us, unconvincing.

A murmur ripples through the assembled guests. The vicar straightens, preparing for the bride's entrance. I turn toward the doorway, my heart quickening against my will.

The doors remain closed.

I check my timepiece. Eleanor is punctual to a fault. She should be here.

Minutes tick by. The whispering grows more pronounced. I feel countless eyes upon me, sympathetic, curious, pitying.

Not again.

The thought claws at me, unwelcome and persistent.

Not again.

My collar feels suddenly tight. "Henry—"

"She'll be here," he assures me quietly. "There's likely a simple explanation."

"Of course." I force my expression to remain neutral, though inside, a storm brews. Fool. Did I learn nothing from Seraphina? Did I truly believe this time would be different? Eleanor seemed so genuine, so unlike the calculated charm of my former fiancée, but perhaps that was merely a different type of deception.

The church doors finally swing open. My breath catches—then releases in confusion.

Not Eleanor in her bridal finery, but a red-faced housemaid rushing down the aisle, her cap askew, her apron stained. The congregation gasps collectively at this breach of decorum.

"Your Grace!" she calls, still several feet away, seemingly oblivious to the sacred setting or the impropriety of shouting at a duke. "Begging your pardon, Your Grace!"

I step forward, my pulse hammering against my temples. "What is the meaning of this?"

The girl drops into a clumsy curtsy, panting for breath. "It's Lady Eleanor, Your Grace. There's been a terrible outbreak at Ravensbrook Hall—influenza, they're saying. Half the household's abed with it."

Someone gasps behind me. The girl continues, her words tumbling over one another.

"She was tending to the McBride family, Your Grace—they took ill first. Said she couldn't leave them suffering when she knew what to do. But then yesterday she started with the fever herself, and now she's—" The maid's voice breaks. "She's very ill, Your Grace. Lady Victoria sent me to tell you. They couldn't leave her side to come themselves."

Relief and terror war within me. Not betrayal then, but devotion—foolish, reckless devotion to a tenant family that could cost her... I cannot complete the thought.

"How bad?" I demand, my voice dropping to a pitch only Henry and the maid can hear.

The girl's eyes fill with tears. "Dr. Bennett says it's grave, Your Grace. Very grave indeed. Lady Eleanor's fever is dangerously high, and she's—she's not always making sense when she speaks."

The room spins briefly. Grave. The word echoes in my mind. I had prepared myself for abandonment, for the familiar sting of rejection—not this. Not Eleanor lying delirious with fever while I stood waiting in a church, questioning her character.

Henry's hand is on my shoulder, steadying me. "Sebastian—"

"Have my carriage brought around immediately," I command, cutting through his concern. "Tell the vicar to dismiss the guests with my apologies."

The maid bobs another curtsy. "Yes, Your Grace. Right away, Your Grace."

As she scurries away, Henry leans closer. "What are you planning to do?"

I meet his concerned gaze, something resolute hardening within me. "I'm going to Ravensbrook Hall."

"Of course," Henry nods. "Anne and I will follow—"

"No." I shake my head. "Stay with your family. I'll send word when I know more."

The congregation buzzes with speculation as I stride down the aisle, shedding the carefully constructed poise of the Duke of Westmoreland with each step. In this moment, I am simply Sebastian—a man who has only just realized how terrifying it is to care deeply for someone who might be slipping away.

I race through the countryside, the drumming of hooves matching the frantic beat of my heart. The journey to Ravensbrook Hall has never seemed so interminable. My driver pushes the horses to their limits at my command, yet still I lean forward in the carriage as if my posture might somehow propel us faster.

The verdant Yorkshire landscape blurs past, unnoted and unappreciated. My thoughts remain fixed on Eleanor—her quiet smile, her downcast eyes that light with unexpected passion when she speaks of music, her gentle way of slipping into the background of any gathering. *How did I not see her worth sooner? How could I have been so blind?*

As we approach the long drive to Ravensbrook, I catch sight of a carriage traveling in the opposite direction. Something in its haste draws my attention. I pound my walking stick against the roof of my own conveyance.

"Stop! Pull alongside that carriage!"

My driver complies, cutting across the road to intercept the departing vehicle. I recognize the Hartwood crest emblazoned on its side instantly.

"Halt!" I call out, my voice carrying the unmistakable authority of my station.

The other driver pulls his team to a stop. I leap from my carriage before it has fully settled, striding toward the Hartwood conveyance with mounting fury as I comprehend what I'm witnessing.

Lord Hartwood's startled face appears at the window, followed by Lady Victoria's pinched expression. The carriage door swings open.

"Westmoreland," Lord Hartwood says, his discomfort evident. "We did not expect to see you on the road."

"Clearly not," I reply, ice coating each syllable. "I find it rather remarkable to see Eleanor's family abandoning Ravensbrook when I've just been informed she lies gravely ill."

Victoria leans forward. "The illness has spread throughout the household. Dr. Bennett advised us to remove ourselves before we too succumb."

"And Eleanor?" I demand. "What of her?"

Lord Hartwood clears his throat. "The doctor is attending her. We've left instructions with the remaining staff."

"Remaining staff?" My voice drops dangerously low. "How many remain to care for your daughter?"

An uncomfortable silence stretches between us. Finally, Victoria speaks. "Her lady's maid refused to leave. Most others have fallen ill or fled out of fear of contagion."

"I see." The words emerge with deadly calm, belying the tempest within. "So you leave your daughter—your sister—virtually alone as she fights for her life?"

"Now see here," Lord Hartwood bristles. "I have other children to consider. Victoria has her own children waiting in York. We cannot all risk exposure for one—"

"For one what?" I interrupt, stepping closer. "One daughter? One sister? One human being who deserves your care and loyalty?"

"You do not understand," Victoria interjects. "Eleanor would want us to protect ourselves. She's always put others before herself—"

"Yes," I cut in, "a quality apparently not shared by her family."

Lord Hartwood's face flushes with anger. "Mind your tone, Westmoreland. You may be a Duke, but you overstep. Eleanor is my daughter—"

"A fact you seem to have conveniently forgotten," I retort. "Tell me, Lord Hartwood, was it also for Eleanor's benefit that you routinely diminished her worth in company? That you spoke of her as a burden, an unmarriageable disappointment? I witnessed your surprise when I asked for her hand—as if the notion that someone might value her was inconceivable."

Victoria gasps. "That's unfair! We've only wanted Eleanor to be realistic about her prospects—"

"Her prospects?" I laugh, the sound devoid of humor. "Her prospects include becoming a duchess, yet here you are, fleeing her sickbed on her wedding day."

"The wedding can wait," Lord Hartwood mutters, refusing to meet my gaze. "If she recovers—"

"When," I correct him sharply. "*When* she recovers. And she shall do so without the comfort of her family, it seems."

"We've left money for additional nursing if needed," Victoria offers weakly.

"How magnanimous." My contempt is undisguised. "Now, if you'll excuse me, I intend to be at my fiancée's side, where her family should be."

I step back from the carriage, my disgust palpable. "Drive on," I command their coachman. "I wouldn't want to delay your escape any further."

The wheels begin to turn, and I watch with undisguised scorn as they continue down the drive, not a single face looking back toward the home where Eleanor lies suffering. I return to my own carriage and snap orders to proceed to Ravensbrook Hall immediately.

Upon arrival, the manor's hushed silence strikes me as ominous. No footmen appear to greet the carriage. No butler stands at attention. I leap from the conveyance and take the entrance stairs two at a time, pushing open the massive doors myself.

"Hello?" My voice echoes through the cavernous entrance hall. "Is anyone here?"

Silence answers me, feeding the terror that has been building since the church. I race across the marble floor, calling again, louder now. "Hello! I require assistance immediately!"

Nothing. The great house feels abandoned, tomb-like. Panic rises in my throat as I take the grand staircase at a run, my footsteps thundering against the wood.

"Eleanor!" I shout, propriety forgotten. "Eleanor!"

I reach the landing, disoriented by my unfamiliarity with the house layout. *Which room is hers? How will I find her in this labyrinth?*

A shuffling sound draws my attention to the right corridor. A disheveled figure emerges from a doorway, hair escaping its cap, apron stained with what appears to be broth and medicinal powders.

"Wallace?" I recognize Eleanor's lady's maid instantly, though her appearance is so altered by exhaustion I might have passed her on the street without notice.

"Yer Grace!" Relief floods her weary features, her Scottish brogue thickened by emotion. "Oh, thank the heavens! I didna know how much longer I could manage alone."

"Where is she?" I demand, crossing to her in three long strides.

"This way, Yer Grace." Wallace turns back toward the door she emerged from. "She's been callin' for ye, though I wasna sure ye'd know yet about the illness—"

"I came as soon as I heard," I assure her, following close behind. "Has there been any change?"

Wallace's tired face grows grim. "The fever rages still. Dr.

Bennett was here this mornin' but had other patients to attend. Said he'd return by evenin' if he could."

She pushes open the door to Eleanor's chamber, and I step across the threshold. The room is dimly lit, heavy curtains drawn against the daylight. The air hangs thick with the smell of illness—camphor and perspiration and medicinal tinctures.

My eyes adjust slowly to the gloom, seeking the bed that dominates the center of the room. When I finally see her, my legs nearly give way beneath me.

Eleanor lies motionless amid rumpled bedding, her skin so pale it seems translucent against the dark sheets. Her normally severe hairstyle has been undone, dark tendrils plastered against her temples with sweat. Her chest rises and falls in shallow, rapid breaths.

She looks impossibly small, fragile in a way I've never associated with her quiet strength. This cannot be my Eleanor—the woman who challenged me with surprising wit, who tended sick tenants with no thought for herself.

I move toward the bed as if pulled by an invisible force, my knees finally buckling at her side.

CHAPTER SIXTEEN
GRASS IN YOUR HAIR
THE DUKE OF WESTMORELAND

I pace the corridor outside Eleanor's chamber, my boot heels marking a relentless rhythm against the polished floor. Three days. Three interminable days of watching her life balance on the edge of a knife. Each hour that passes without improvement drives the blade deeper into my own heart.

Dr. Bennett emerges from the sickroom, closing the door quietly behind him. The grim set of his mouth tells me everything before he utters a single word.

"Your Grace." He bows slightly. "I have administered another dose of willow bark tea, but I fear it has little effect on her fever."

"There must be something more we can do." My voice sounds foreign to my own ears—ragged, desperate, lacking all the cool arrogance that has been my armor for so long.

The physician's eyes hold the weary resignation of a man who has delivered too many death sentences. "If she has not broken the fever by now, Your Grace, I must prepare you for the likelihood that she will not survive the night."

The corridor seems suddenly airless. I brace my hand against the wall, steadying myself.

"I have seen the strongest men felled by this influenza, and Lady Eleanor has fought valiantly, but—"

"She is stronger than anyone knows," I cut him off, unwilling to hear the rest.

Dr. Bennett studies me with professional concern. "And how are you feeling, Your Grace? You have scarcely left this corridor in three days."

"I am tired, nothing more." I run a hand across my unshaven jaw. "But I feel quite well, physically."

"You must take care of yourself as well. The illness—"

"I am fine," I snap, then immediately regret my harshness. "Forgive me, Doctor. I am merely... concerned."

He nods, understanding in his eyes. "I shall return in the morning. Send for me immediately if there is any change."

I watch him descend the grand staircase, his medical bag swinging heavily at his side, before turning back to Eleanor's door. Wallace, Eleanor's maid, slips past me with fresh water and linens. Her eyes are red-rimmed from exhaustion and worry.

I resume my pacing, each turn bringing me to the window that overlooks the gardens. Summer blooms in riotous color below, oblivious to the battle being waged within these walls.

How strange that the world continues on, heedless of the fact that Eleanor might be leaving it.

A crash from within the chamber shatters my thoughts. The unmistakable sound of shattering porcelain is followed by Wallace's panicked scream.

"Your Grace! I don't think she's breathing!"

I burst through the door, nearly tearing it from its hinges. Wallace stands frozen beside the bed, water pooling at her feet among the shards of a broken pitcher. Her hands cover her mouth, her eyes wide with horror.

"Move!" I push past her, dropping to my knees beside the bed.

Eleanor lies still, *so* still. Her skin bears the unnatural pallor of alabaster, her lips tinged blue. The vibrant, grass-stained woman who laughed in the sunlight seems a distant memory, replaced by this fragile shell.

I press my fingers to her throat, searching desperately for a pulse. Is there the faintest flutter beneath my fingertips, or merely the tremor of my own hand?

"Eleanor," I whisper, then louder, "Eleanor!"

I take her hand between mine. It is small and cool, the skin dry with fever. "Breathe, Eleanor. You must breathe."

Behind me, Wallace sobs quietly.

"Fetch more cold water." I order without turning. "And send for Dr. Bennett's return—Immediately."

The maid hurries from the room, her footsteps receding rapidly down the hallway.

Alone with Eleanor, I press her hand to my cheek. "You cannot leave me," I say, my voice breaking on the words. "Not when we have only just found each other."

I smooth a damp strand of hair from her forehead. Even in illness, there is something about her face that captivates me—a quality I was too blind to recognize when we first met.

"I remember the first moment I truly saw you," I whisper, my thumb tracing the delicate line of her wrist. "Not at the ball, not in your father's drawing room, but in that sun-drenched field. You had grass in your hair—ridiculous, beautiful green blades tangled in those dark locks. Your cheeks were flushed with embarrassment, but your eyes... your eyes held such life."

My vision blurs. I blink rapidly, unwilling to relinquish my gaze upon her face even for a moment.

"And when I pulled that grass from your hair, your skin beneath my fingertips... I felt something I cannot explain. As if some missing piece of myself had suddenly been found." A ragged laugh escapes me. "Imagine that. The Duke of Westmoreland, undone by a few blades of grass."

I lean closer, my forehead nearly touching hers. "I have been surrounded by beauty my entire life, Eleanor. Empty, meaningless beauty that demanded admiration but offered nothing in return. But you... you hide your beauty—not behind fans or coy smiles, but beneath a quiet dignity that I find myself desperate to uncover."

Her chest rises and falls so shallowly that I can barely detect the movement.

"You must fight," I plead, gripping her hand tighter. "You are stronger than you believe. Stronger than this illness. Stronger than the doubts that have shadowed you all your life."

I press my lips to her knuckles, no longer caring if anyone should enter and witness this display of naked emotion from a man who has prided himself on his reserve.

"I cannot wait to marry you, Eleanor Hartwood. I cannot wait to discover every hidden melody in your heart. I have fallen in love with you—not despite your differences from other women, but because of them. I love your honesty, your kindness—I love the woman who lies in the grass to watch clouds, who cares for farmers' children, who runs from ballrooms when they become too much."

My voice cracks completely, unraveling into a desperate whisper.

"Please, Eleanor. I love you. Come back to me."

I wipe away the tears that have betrayed me, embarrassed by this display even with no witnesses save the unconscious woman before me. My fingers curl around Eleanor's delicate hand once more, bringing it close to my chest where my heart hammers against my ribs with relentless force.

"I am not leaving this spot until you open your eyes," I whisper, my voice thick with emotion I no longer care to disguise. "Do you hear me, Eleanor? I will wait here for as long as it takes."

I feel it then—so faint I might have imagined it. A twitch. The slightest movement against my palm. I freeze, scarcely daring to breathe.

There. Again. Her fingers curl weakly into mine.

"Eleanor?" My voice trembles with desperate hope.

I lean over her, my face mere inches from hers. Her eyelids flutter, fighting their own weight.

"Fight, Eleanor," I whisper urgently against her ear, my breath stirring the dark strands of her hair. "Fight! Come back to me."

The rise and fall of her chest grows stronger, more deliberate. Her head turns slightly toward my voice, as if seeking its source.

"Sebastian?" Her voice is barely audible, a ghost of sound that nonetheless crashes through me like thunder.

I drop my forehead to the bedsheets beside her, overcome. My shoulders shake with silent, heaving sobs that I can no longer contain. She spoke. She lives. She knows me.

"Sebastian?" she calls again, slightly stronger now. "Is that truly you?"

I lift my head, not bothering to hide the tears that streak my face. "I am here, Eleanor. I have been here."

Her eyes open, unfocused and fever-bright, before sliding closed again. She draws a labored breath. "I thought... I was dreaming."

"Not a dream." I press her hand to my lips. "I am real. And you—you are coming back to me."

"The wedding." Her words slur together slightly. "I missed... our wedding."

A laugh escapes me—part joy, part lingering fear. "The wedding matters not. Only you matter."

She struggles to open her eyes again, blinking slowly in the dim light of the chamber. Her cracked lips part in a weak attempt at a smile. "You... waited."

"I would wait forever." The words emerge raw and honest.

Her free hand moves then, so slowly, lifting from the counterpane. For a moment it hovers, wavering with effort, before settling atop my head where it rests against her side. Her fingers thread weakly into my hair, the gesture so tender it nearly undoes me completely.

"You are... here." Her voice holds wonder, as if she cannot believe I have remained at her bedside through this ordeal.

"Where else would I be?" I ask softly, turning my face to look into her eyes. "You are to be my wife."

The ghost of a smile touches her lips. "Not very... practical... of you."

Even now, even here, she remembers my cold words about our arrangement. Shame burns through me.

"Practicality be damned," I murmur, shifting upward. I cradle her face between my hands, feeling the lingering heat of fever against my palms. Her eyes widen slightly as I bend toward her.

My lips press gently against her forehead, lingering there as I breathe in the scent of her—no longer the sharp tang of illness, but something softer, something uniquely Eleanor beginning to emerge once again.

The door opens behind me, and Wallace's startled gasp breaks the moment. I turn, not releasing Eleanor's hand.

"She's awake!" The maid clutches the fresh pitcher to her chest, water sloshing over the rim in her excitement. "Oh, praise the saints above! She's awake!"

"Fetch some broth," I order, my voice steady despite the tempest of emotions raging within me. "And tell the messenger to inform Dr. Bennett that Lady Eleanor has broken her fever."

Wallace hurries from the room, her exclamations of joy echoing down the corridor.

I turn back to Eleanor, who watches me with half-lidded eyes, exhaustion already pulling her back toward sleep—but natural sleep now, healing rather than ominous.

"Do not leave me," she murmurs, her fingers tightening fractionally around mine.

"Never." I press my lips to her knuckles. "Rest now. I will be here when you wake."

Her eyes drift closed, but the faintest smile remains upon her lips as her breathing deepens into the rhythm of sleep.

I look upward, toward the ornate ceiling and beyond to whatever power might reside above. No prayer forms upon my lips—I have not been a praying man these many years—but gratitude fills me nonetheless, overwhelming in its intensity.

She lives. She will recover. And when she is well enough, I will make her my wife—not for practicality or convenience or the succession of my title, but because I cannot imagine my life without her in it.

I settle into the chair beside her bed, still holding her hand, prepared to keep my vigil through the night.

This time, I will be the first thing she sees when she fully opens her eyes.

TEN YEARS LATER
THE DUCHESS OF WESTMORELAND

I lean back against the trunk of the ancient oak tree, its gnarled branches providing a blessed respite from the summer sun that beats down upon Waltham Manor. The white canvas of the tent billows gently in the afternoon breeze, creating dancing patterns of light and shadow across the precisely trimmed lawn. The sound of children's laughter mingles with birdsong, creating a symphony that swells my heart with contentment.

"Mama! Did you see? I knocked down all the pins!" Marcus shouts, his nine-year-old face alight with the triumph of victory. His dark hair—so like his father's—falls across his forehead in an unruly wave that no amount of combing seems to tame.

"I saw, darling," I call back, unable to keep the pride from my voice. "Your aim improves each day."

William, not to be outdone by his elder brother, seizes the wooden ball with determined hands. At seven, he possesses none of Marcus's natural athletic grace but compensates with a fierce determination that makes my chest tighten with recognition. It is the same resolve I once channeled solely into my music, before I learned I might apply it to other aspects of life as well.

"My turn!" he announces with grave solemnity, his brow furrowing in concentration as he positions himself for his throw.

Near the refreshment table, Anne's voice rises above the general hum of conversation. "Absolutely not, Sophie. Twenty-two is far too young to tie yourself to a man of forty-five, regardless of how many times you declare yourself in love!"

"You cannot understand," Sophie retorts, her twenty-two-year-old dignity wounded. "Lord Eddington is different from other gentlemen. He values my mind."

"I suspect he values a great many things besides your mind," Anne mutters, glancing heavenward as if seeking divine intervention. "Catherine and Margaret both waited until at least three-and-twenty before marrying. There is wisdom in patience."

My attention shifts to the far edge of the lawn, where Sebastian kneels beside our Violet. At five years old, she remains the most delicate of our children, with my unremarkable brown hair but her father's expressive eyes. Sebastian's hands—those elegant, strong fingers that coax such emotion from piano keys—now gently guide hers around the wooden ball.

TEN YEARS LATER

"Like this, poppet," he instructs, his voice carrying on the breeze. "Keep your wrist firm but not tense. Now, follow through with your arm..."

Together, they release the ball, sending it rolling smoothly down the grass to topple three of the wooden pins. Violet's squeal of delight pierces the air, and Sebastian sweeps her into his arms, spinning her until her muslin dress billows like a cloud around her tiny legs.

How different is this Sebastian from the cold, arrogant nobleman who once asked for my hand with such detached practicality. The man who spins our daughter beneath the summer sky bears only the faintest resemblance to that earlier incarnation—like a watercolor painting left in the rain, his sharp edges have softened, his severe lines blurred into something warmer, more vibrant.

And I—I am no longer the shadow who drifted through drawing rooms unnoticed, head bowed and voice muted. No longer the plain, unremarkable sister whose only distinction lay in the music she played when no one was listening.

Last week, I hosted a musical evening that drew compliments from the Countess of Westham herself. "Such conversation, my dear Eleanor," she'd said, patting my hand. "One never leaves Waltham Manor without having engaged in the most stimulating discourse."

I'd smiled and thanked her, not revealing how those words would have once seemed an impossible fantasy. The Eleanor of ten years past would never have commanded a salon of thirty guests, steering conversation from literature to politics with a confidence that now feels as natural as breathing.

My gaze returns to Sebastian as he releases Violet to play with her cousins. The afternoon sun catches in his hair, illuminating threads of silver at his temples that only enhance his appearance. Unlike many men who rage against such signs of aging, Sebastian wears his years with the same elegant insouciance with which he wears his perfectly tailored jacket.

Tonight, when the children are abed and we retire to our chamber, I will tell him about the child growing beneath my heart. Our fourth. I touch my still-flat stomach, imagining his reaction—that slow, devastating smile that still makes my breath catch after a decade of marriage.

My mind drifts to our wedding night, to the uncertainty that had plagued me as we stood on opposite sides of that massive bed. How foolish those fears seem now. I recall the gentleness of his first touch, the reverence with which he'd kissed each inch of my skin as if discovering some priceless treasure. The memory of his whispered words—"You are exquisite, Eleanor"—still has the power to send heat coursing through my veins.

That night, as passion overtook restraint and we moved together in the ancient rhythm of lovers, I had discovered a truth that has only deepened with each passing year: there exists no greater intimacy than when two souls find themselves truly seen by another.

I watch him now as he moves across the lawn, stopping to ruffle William's hair, to adjust Marcus's stance, to accept a flower crown from Violet with grave ceremony. My husband. *My Sebastian*. The man who showed me that beauty dwells not in the perfect symmetry of features but in the connection of kindred spirits.

The man who taught me that music exists not only in the notes I play, but in the cadence of children's laughter, in the rhythm of shared breaths in the darkness, in the silent communication of eyes that meet across crowded rooms.

Sebastian looks up suddenly, as if sensing my gaze upon him. Our eyes lock, and even from this distance, I see his expression soften. He inclines his head slightly—a private gesture, a question. I smile in response, and he nods, understanding passing between us without a single word spoken...

TEN YEARS BEFORE

Two weeks after I recovered from the sickness, before our families and friends, we are married. The church is adorned with garlands of white roses and sprigs of lavender—my favorite. I stand at the altar beside Sebastian, watching the morning light filter through the stained glass windows, casting kaleidoscope patterns across his handsome face. His eyes never leave mine as we speak our vows, his voice strong and unwavering, mine soft but steady. When he slides the gold band onto my finger, I feel the warmth of his touch linger, as though branding me as his own.

I cannot believe the change in Sebastian. Gone is the arrogant, cold man I first encountered. In his place stands a husband—

my husband—attentive and kind, anticipating my every whim before I can even express it. After the ceremony, he keeps his hand at the small of my back, a protective gesture that sends shivers of delight through me. When someone offers congratulations, his pride is evident in the way he introduces me as "my wife, the Duchess of Westmoreland," the words rolling off his tongue as though he has been waiting his entire life to say them.

He did indeed not leave my side during my illness. The memories of those fevered days remain fragmented, like shattered glass—disconnected images and sensations. The cool cloth on my forehead. The bitter taste of medicine. The sound of someone praying. And always, Sebastian's voice, cutting through the fog of delirium, anchoring me to the world of the living. "Stay with me, Eleanor. Please. I cannot lose you now."

When I finally opened my eyes, weak but alive, he was there, slumped in a chair beside my bed, his face unshaven, his clothing rumpled. The moment he realized I was awake, the transformation in his countenance was extraordinary—like watching the sun break through storm clouds. He wept then, unashamed, clutching my hand to his lips, whispering words I was too weak to fully comprehend but whose meaning I felt in my very soul.

The marriage breakfast passes in a whirlwind of faces and voices. I feel oddly detached, as though watching myself from a distance—smiling, accepting congratulations, cutting the elaborate cake with Sebastian's hand steady over mine. Lady Anne embraces me with genuine affection, whispering,

"Welcome to the family, sister." My own sisters look on with expressions of astonishment, clearly bewildered by the devotion Sebastian shows me. Even Father seems stunned, though he masks it with jovial bluster, claiming he always knew I would make an excellent match.

Now alone, Sebastian and I stand on opposite sides of the bed in our chamber at Waltham Manor. The wedding night. *My wedding night.* The phrase echoes in my mind, both thrilling and terrifying. The room is lit only by the soft glow of candles and the dying embers in the fireplace. The grand four-poster bed between us seems like both a barrier and an invitation.

I wear a nightgown of the finest silk, so thin it feels like wearing moonlight. I had blushed furiously when my sisters presented it to me, Victoria declaring with a wicked smile that "the Duke will appreciate the expense." Now, I am acutely conscious of how it clings to my modest curves, how the candlelight renders it nearly transparent.

Sebastian stands across from me in his night shift, and I cannot help but stare. In the flickering light, he appears almost otherworldly—the hard planes of his chest visible through the fine linen, his dark hair tousled from removing his formal attire. His eyes, usually so controlled and guarded, now burn with an intensity that steals my breath.

"Eleanor," he whispers, and just my name on his lips sounds like a caress.

I am frozen, caught between desire and uncertainty. *What does one do when a dream suddenly manifests in reality? How does one embrace joy after resigning oneself to its absence?*

"I never thought—" I begin, then stop.

"What, love? Tell me."

"I never thought anyone would look at me the way you are looking at me now."

His expression softens. "Then everyone else was blind."

We move toward each other, drawn like magnets, until we meet in the middle of the bed. The mattress dips beneath our weight as we kneel, face to face. Sebastian reaches out, his fingers tracing the curve of my cheek with such tenderness I feel I might shatter.

"May I kiss my wife?" he asks, his voice rough with emotion.

I nod, not trusting my voice, and close my eyes as his lips touch mine.

The kiss begins gently, a mere whisper of contact. His lips are warm and surprisingly soft against mine. I feel his restraint, his careful control, and something within me yearns to break it. Tentatively, I press closer, my hands finding their way to his shoulders.

Something shifts then—a dam breaking. Sebastian makes a sound deep in his throat, and suddenly his arms are around me, pulling me flush against him. The kiss deepens, transforms from sweet to consuming. His tongue traces the seam of my lips, and I open to him instinctively, a soft gasp escaping me at the intimate contact.

"I've wanted this—wanted you—since I pulled grass from your

hair," he murmurs against my mouth. "My beautiful, surprising Eleanor."

His hands slide down my back, leaving trails of heat through the thin silk. I arch against him, suddenly desperate for more of his touch. My own boldness shocks me—I, who have always been so proper, so contained, now trembling with need in my husband's arms.

"Sebastian," I breathe, my voice unrecognizable even to my own ears. "Please."

He groans at my plea, his control visibly fraying. "Tell me what you want, love. I would give you the world."

"I want you. Just you."

Sebastian peels my chemise back with exquisite slowness, exposing my breasts to the cool night air. I gasp as he begins his reverent exploration, his lips and tongue paying such devoted attention to each peak and nipple that I can scarcely breathe. My body arches involuntarily toward his touch, a flame igniting deep within me, spreading outward until I'm consumed by it.

"I cannot—" I whisper, my voice breaking as his mouth closes over one sensitive peak. The sensation is almost too much to bear, this sweet torment that has me trembling beneath him. I thread my fingers through his dark hair, holding him to me even as I feel myself unraveling. My body, which has always been so contained, so controlled, now betrays me completely, responding to his every caress with a fervor I never knew I possessed.

"Sebastian, please," I whimper, not even knowing what I'm begging for, only that this burning need inside me must find release before it consumes me entirely.

He tells me to brace for the pain, and I do not know what to expect—but when he enters me, I feel complete, full, and the intimacy unravels me in ways I never imagined possible. *How could this be?* This sacred connection between two people … so … utterly … sublime.

The initial discomfort gives way to something profound and overwhelming, as he continues to kiss me deeply, lovingly, his lips capturing my gasps as if they were precious things to be treasured. Each gentle movement builds something within me—a tension, a yearning, a climbing sensation that blooms from deep inside like the most exquisite music crescendoing toward its climax. My hands clutch at his shoulders, anchoring myself as this unfamiliar pleasure spreads through my trembling body. Sebastian finds his own pleasure, his breathing ragged against my neck, and in that moment of shared vulnerability, I feel truly seen for perhaps the first time in my life.

I lie in Sebastian's arms, utterly transformed. The woman I was mere hours ago—hesitant, uncertain—seems a stranger to me now. In her place is this new creature, baptized in pleasure, reborn in the sanctuary of my husband's embrace.

"You're trembling," Sebastian whispers, his breath warm against my temple. His hand traces idle patterns on my bare shoulder, each touch igniting renewed shivers across my skin.

"Am I?" I manage, though I can feel the fine tremors coursing through my limbs. "I cannot seem to stop."

The bedsheets are tangled around us, the fine linen cool against our heated skin. Outside, rain has begun to fall, pattering softly against the windowpanes—nature's gentle applause for what has transpired between us.

Sebastian shifts, propping himself on one elbow to gaze down at me. In the faint glow from the dying fire, his face is all planes and shadows, his eyes dark pools in which I could drown willingly. The look he gives me—tender, reverent, hungry still—draws a soft gasp from my lips.

"Do you know how beautiful you are?" His fingers trace the curve of my cheek, my jaw, the column of my throat. "Not just here—" his hand drifts lower, palm flattening against my sternum where my heart thunders beneath his touch, "—but here, most of all."

I catch his hand in mine, pressing it more firmly against my heart. "You have branded me, Your Grace. I shall never be the same."

"Sebastian," he corrects, his voice rough with emotion. "Always Sebastian when we're alone."

"Sebastian," I whisper, his name a prayer on my lips.

He lowers his mouth to mine, and I open to him instinctively, as though we have been lovers for centuries rather than hours. The kiss deepens, slow and thorough, rekindling the embers that never truly died. His hand slides lower, spanning my waist, pulling me closer until every inch of us touches—chest to chest, hip to hip, his hardness pressing insistently against my thigh.

"Again?" I breathe against his mouth, both question and invitation.

His answering smile is wicked, the smile of a man who has discovered treasure beyond imagining. "Always. Forever. If you'll have me."

"I am yours." The simplicity of the statement belies its profound truth. I *am* his, utterly and completely, in ways I never imagined possible.

This time when he enters me, there is no pain—only the exquisite sensation of completeness, of being filled by the man I love. For I do love him. The realization washes over me with the force of a tidal wave, stealing my breath. I love him with a ferocity that should terrify me, yet instead fills me with courage I never knew I possessed.

I arch beneath him, meeting each thrust, hands grasping at his shoulders, his back, anywhere I can reach. Gone is my earlier shyness; in its place burns a bold desire to claim and be claimed. I lift my hips higher, taking him deeper, and am rewarded with a groan that seems torn from his very soul.

We move together, finding a rhythm as natural as the tides. I marvel at how my body knows what to do, how to respond, how to climb toward that pinnacle I now recognize awaits us both. Sebastian watches my face with an intensity that would once have made me turn away in embarrassment. Now, I meet his gaze boldly, letting him see the pleasure he brings me written plainly across my features.

His pace quickens, and I sense he nears his completion. Yet he holds back, his jaw clenched with the effort of restraint, and I understand he waits for me. The realization—that even in this, he puts my pleasure before his own—sends me careening over the edge. Wave after wave of ecstasy crashes through me, my body clenching around him, my voice crying out his name as though summoning him to follow.

And follow he does, his release coming moments after mine, his face transformed by pleasure so acute it resembles pain. He collapses beside me, gathering me close, our heartbeats gradually slowing in tandem.

"I never knew," I whisper against his chest. "I never knew it could be like this."

He presses a kiss to my forehead. "Nor I, love. You have unmade me."

We lie entwined, silence stretching between us like a silken thread. But it is not the awkward silence of strangers; rather, the peaceful quiet of souls who have found their harbor after long journeys apart.

"I fought it, you know," Sebastian says finally, his voice low in the darkness. "From the moment I saw you on that veranda. Something in me recognized you—not just your face or form, but your soul. It terrified me."

I lift my head to look at him. "Why?"

"Because I had resolved never to love again. To marry for practicality, for continuation of the bloodline, for any reason but the one that had once left me shattered." His arms tighten around me. "And then there you were, with grass in your hair and uncertainty in your eyes, and all my careful plans unraveled."

My heart swells, pushing against my ribs as though trying to break free and merge with his. "I love you, Sebastian. I thought myself incapable of inspiring such feelings in another, yet here we are."

"Here we are indeed." He cups my face between his palms, thumbs brushing away tears I hadn't realized I'd shed. "I love you, Eleanor Hanbury, Duchess of Westmoreland. Not for your beauty, though you are beautiful beyond measure to me. Not for your lineage or connections or any worldly consideration. I love you for your courage, your kindness, your passion that you hide from the world but show to me. I love you for making me believe in love again when I thought that part of me long dead."

I press my lips to his, sealing his declaration with a kiss that speaks when words fail. In this bed, in this man's arms, I have found not just pleasure, but home—the place where I am truly seen, truly cherished, truly loved.

THE END

YOU MIGHT ALSO LIKE

BEST-SELLER!
A MARRIAGE OF MISMATCH

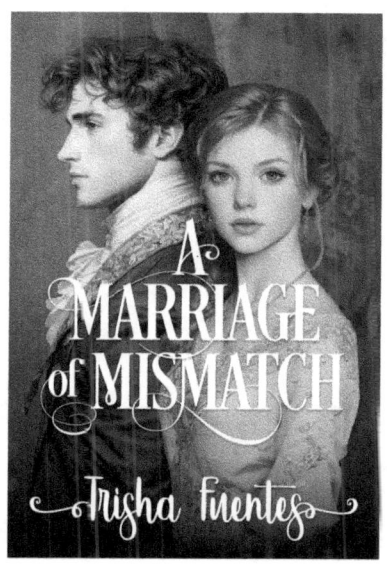

A SCANDALOUS REGENCY ROMANCE

When rebellious Viscount Oliver Thorne is caught in a scandalous situation, his family forces him into a marriage of convenience with the prim and proper Lady Eleanor Cavendish. Oliver is determined to make Eleanor's life miserable, but as they spend more time together, he begins to question his preconceived notions. Will their clashing personalities lead to love or disaster?

Key Features:

- Historical Romance: Immerse yourself in the glamorous world of Regency England.

- Forbidden Love: Explore the tension between a rebellious Viscount and a proper Lady.
- Unexpected Twist: Discover a heartwarming tale of love and redemption.

Get lost in a world of passion, intrigue, and unforgettable characters.

Available in

Ebook & Paperback

INK AND AFFECTION

A SCANDALOUS WIDOW. A DESPERATE LORD. A CONTRACT THAT IGNITES FORBIDDEN AFFECTION.

Dive into "Ink and Affection," a captivating tale of a marriage forged in pragmatism, but destined for something far more profound.

Lord Nathaniel Ravenswood faces ruin unless he secures an heir. Lady Sophia Harrington, a widowed beauty with a scandalous past and a fortune to invest, offers an unconventional solution: a marriage of convenience.

Their meticulously crafted contract—separate bed-chambers, shared finances, and a strict "no emotional demands" clause—seems foolproof. But as spring awakens, so does an undeniable attraction that threatens to shatter their carefully constructed walls.

A Marriage of Convenience Regency Romance

Available in

Ebook & Paperback

A HEART'S WAGER

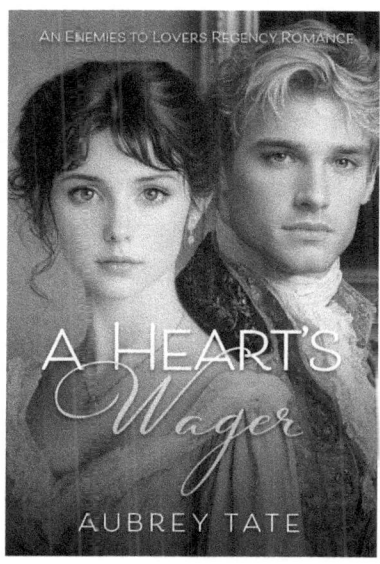

Miss Georgiana Hartwell may be the richest heiress in London, but her family's fortune—built on revolutionary steam-powered furnaces that transformed England's metalworking industry—can't buy her acceptance among the ton. Educated in business rather than needlepoint, Georgiana harbors ambitions to expand her late father's manufacturing empire, even as society expects her to simply marry well and relinquish control to a husband.

Viscount James Westbury, with his impeccable lineage and notorious charm, appears to be the perfect aristocrat—until one ventures inside his empty coffers. After a disastrous night at the gaming tables leaves him on the verge of complete ruin, he sets his sights on the merchant's daughter and her unseemly fortune as his salvation.

When Georgiana publicly humiliates the viscount after discovering his mercenary intentions, a compromising situation forces them into a sham courtship to avoid scandal. Trapped in each other's company, James begins to admire the brilliant mind behind Georgiana's unusual upbringing, while she glimpses the honorable man beneath his rakish facade—a man who sacrifices everything to care for his sisters after their father's disgrace.

An Enemies to Lovers Regency Romance

Available in

Ebook & Paperback

A SPANISH BRIDE FOR STRATHMORE

FROM SUN-DRENCHED SPAIN TO THE ICY HALLS OF AN ENGLISH EARL...

Catalina Esperanza Navarro had been shielded in comfort in Barcelona which had been bracing itself against the turmoil of Napoleonic conquest. As the cherished daughter of a shrewd Spanish merchant, her life had been one of privilege. But when the shadow of war had fallen across Spain, her father, desperate to secure her future, had orchestrated a transaction that sent her across the seas.

Hugh Wentworth, the Earl of Strathmore, a man known for his icy control, desperately needed a wealthy bride to save his crumbling estate. Catalina became that bride, a Spanish rose traded for a fortune that shocked London society.

Arriving in England, Catalina was expected to be docile and obedient. But beneath her elegant exterior lay a passionate spirit and carefully guarded secrets. What began as a cold, calculated union soon ignited with a surprising heat as Catalina discovered the cracks in her husband's stoic facade—and the strength she never knew she possessed.

An Arranged Marriage Regency Romance

Available in

Ebook & Paperback

THE AUCTION RIVALS

Miss Victoria Sutton, the orphaned daughter of a renowned art collector, returns to England from Italy to discover her father's debts have forced the auction of his prized collection. Lord Nathaniel Westfield, whose family her father once publicly humiliated in a bidding war, sees the auction as perfect revenge—he plans to acquire the collection for a fraction of its worth, then dismantle it piece by piece.

Forced to live under the same roof when weather delays the auction, their mutual contempt transforms as Victoria recognizes the true appreciation Nathaniel has for the artworks, while he discovers the profound personal connections she has to each piece. When a valuable painting goes missing and Victoria is accused, Nathaniel must choose between his long-harbored resentment and the woman who has unexpectedly captured his heart.

An Enemies to Lovers Regency Romance

Available in

Ebook & Paperback

ABOUT AUBREY

Aubrey Tate is an emerging author of Historical and Regency Romantic Fiction. Aubrey has many writing interests and lives an incognito digital lifestyle.

Aubrey is part of the Ardent Artist Books family and is a published author of several books.

    amazon.com/Ardent-Artist-Books/e/B08BX8F1DZ
    youtube.com/theardentartist

ALSO BY AUBREY

A Marriage of Convenience Regency Romance

Ink and Affection

* * *

An Enemies to Lovers Regency Romance

A Heart's Wager

The Auction Rivals

* * *

An Arranged Marriage Regency Romance

A Spanish Bride for Strathmore

The Duke's Unexpected Heart

and many more, coming soon!

www.ingramcontent.com/pod-product-compliance
Lightning Source LLC
LaVergne TN
LVHW021809060526
838201LV00058B/3301